The Haunting of Upton Manor

David J Cooper

Published by David J Cooper, 2024.

THE HAUNTING OF UPTON MANOR

First edition. April 14, 2024.

Copyright © 2024 David J Cooper.

ISBN: 979-8224638772

Written by David J Cooper.

Also by David J Cooper

Paranormal Mystery Series
The Witch Board
The House of Dolls
The Devil's Coins
The Mirror
The Key
The Reveal

Standalone
The Devil Knows
Se Acabo La Fiesta
Cold Fury
Deadly Encounter
House on the Hill
Diana, Another Royal Scandal
Hanratty - The Final Curtain
The Haunting of Upton Manor

Watch for more at davidjcooperauthorblog.wordpress.com.

Table of Contents

1 1
2 11
3 25
4 39
5 51
6 61
7 71
8 83
9 89
10 101
11 111
12 119
13 131
14 137
15 149

For my dearest friend Janet Buckley.

This book is dedicated to you, a constant source of laughter, support, and love. May its pages remind you of our cherished moments together in Brixham and the depth of our friendship. Thank you for being an irreplaceable part of my life.

David

Preface

In the tranquil embrace of Torbay, where the English Riviera's breathtaking beauty meets the whispering echoes of centuries past, lies Brixham—a picturesque fishing port steeped in history and mystery. Nestled along the rugged coastline, this quaint town boasts a heritage as rich and tumultuous as the tides that rhythmically lap at its shores. Once a notorious haunt for pirates and smugglers, Brixham wears its rugged past like a badge of honour, its storied streets lined with tales of adventure and intrigue.

From the towering cliffs of Berry Head to the enigmatic depths of Sharkham Point, Brixham's landscape is adorned with hidden treasures and secret passages, concealed within the labyrinthine caverns that wind beneath the surface. These subterranean labyrinths, carved by the relentless forces of nature and time, serve as silent witnesses to the town's storied past, inviting intrepid explorers to unravel the mysteries that lie within.

Amidst the maze of history lies Higher Brixham, affectionately known as Cow Town—a quaint quarter where whispers of the past intertwine with the present, and the narrow country lanes seem to breathe with the echoes of bygone eras. At its beating heart stands Fish Town, the bustling harbour that serves as a lifeline to Brixham's seafaring community. Here, the salty tang of the sea mingles with the scent of adventure, weaving a tapestry of sights, sounds, and sensations that captivate the imagination.

But beyond the charming façade lies a darker undercurrent—a realm where folklore and legend converge with the supernatural. Within the shadows of Brixham's storied history, ghostly apparitions glide through the cobblestone streets, their ethereal forms casting eerie shadows in the moonlight. From the haunted halls of Upton Manor to the spectral whispers that drift through the ancient alleyways, the town is alive with the presence of unseen forces, waiting to be discovered by those brave enough to seek them out.

It is within this realm of mystery that my story unfolds—a tale inspired by the chilling encounters of one who resided within the walls of Upton Manor Wing. As the author of this tale, I myself experienced the inexplicable phenomena that haunted the corridors of this historic building, where every creaking floorboard and flickering candle seemed to conceal a secret waiting to be unearthed. From the depths of the sea to the heights of the cliffs, from the secrets buried within the earth to the spirits that roam the night, Brixham is a place where reality and the paranormal intertwine, blurring the lines between the known and the unknown.

Step into the haunting embrace of Brixham's enigmatic history with this gripping tale, inspired by true events. Embark on a mesmerizing journey where the echoes of the past reverberate in every corner, and the secrets of yesteryears lie concealed within the shadows. Prepare to be transported to a realm where whispers of long-forgotten tales linger in the air, beckoning you to unravel their mysteries.

In this atmospheric tale, the lines between the tangible and the spectral blur as the spirits of bygone eras yearn to share their untold stories. Brace yourself for a mesmerising experience where the veil between the living and the dead is as delicate as the shifting sands upon which Brixham rests.

Welcome to a world where history breathes, and the ghosts of the past await their moment to speak. Are you ready to delve into the depths of Brixham's haunted past and uncover the truths that lie hidden beneath its surface? Prepare for an unforgettable adventure where each turn of the page brings you closer to the heart of the mysteries that shroud this ancient town.

Introduction

When acclaimed author Ben Sanders receives an invitation to stay at the infamous Upton Manor, he sees it as the perfect opportunity to find inspiration for his next novel. Little does he know, the shadows that lurk within its walls hold secrets far darker than he could have ever imagined.

After a couple of days at the foreboding estate, he meets Annie, a captivating young woman. Drawn to her enigmatic charm, Ben soon discovers that Annie is no ordinary person.

She is not the only mystery hidden within the manor's confines. Locked away in the depths of its labyrinthine corridors is the elusive Dr. Adrian Kendal, a man shrouded in rumours and whispered tales of madness.

As Ben delves deeper into the secrets of Upton Manor, he finds himself entangled in a web of deceit, betrayal, and supernatural forces beyond his comprehension. With each twist and turn, he uncovers new revelations about the manor's dark history and the sinister Dr. Kendal.

But just when Ben thinks he's uncovered the truth, he's faced with a shocking revelation that turns everything he thought he knew upside down. In a heart-pounding race against time, he must confront the ghosts of the past and unravel the mysteries of Upton Manor before it's too late.

The Haunting of Upton Manor is a gripping tale of suspense, intrigue, and the blurred lines between the living and the dead. Prepare to be spellbound as Ben navigates the twists and turns of this chilling tale, culminating in a surprise ending that will leave you breathless.

1

As the moon hung low in the ink black sky, its silvery light cascaded over the weathered stones of Upton Manor, suffusing the ancient structure with an eerie luminescence. Within the confines of its hallowed walls, Father Gifford, once a bastion of unwavering faith, now grappled with torment wrought by the malevolent entities that lurked in the shadows, their sinister presence palpable in the stagnant air.

Each nightfall brought a new onslaught of spectral whispers and sinister apparitions, driving him to the precipice of despair. The walls, adorned with ivy that seemed to writhe and twist in the ethereal breeze, bore witness to his inner turmoil, their ancient stones echoing with the cries of tortured souls.

Once a sanctuary for the devout, Upton Manor had become a crucible of darkness, its corridors haunted by the ghosts of forgotten sins and unspeakable tragedies. Father Gifford, now a mere shell of his former self, found himself ensnared in a battle for his very soul, his faith tested against the encroaching darkness that threatened to consume him whole.

With each passing night, the malevolent entities within the manor grew stronger, their whispers of temptation and torment echoing through the halls.

Yet, amidst the encroaching shadows, a glimmer of hope flickered within Father Gifford's heart. For though he was besieged by the darkness, he clung to the belief that somewhere within the depths of the manor, salvation awaited, a beacon of light to pierce the veil of night and banish the malevolence that plagued his soul.

He paced the dimly lit corridors, each step echoing like a mournful dirge in the oppressive silence that enveloped him. Whispers, dark and insidious, seemed to emanate from the very stones themselves, their disembodied voices clawing at the fringes of his sanity. The weight of his sins hung heavy upon his shoulders, a suffocating shroud that threatened to consume him whole, dragging him deeper into the abyss of guilt and despair.

With each turn of the corridor, memories of his past transgressions surged forth like a relentless tide, crashing against the fragile barriers of his mind with merciless force. Betrayal, a bitter dagger twisting in his heart; passion, a flame that burned too bright and left nothing but ashes in its wake; and greed, a voracious hunger that gnawed at his soul. These sins intertwined in a macabre tapestry of shame and regret, their tendrils ensnaring him in a web of his own making.

Haunted by the phantoms of his past, Father Gifford stumbled forward, his footsteps faltering as he confronted the spirits that lurked within the recesses of his mind. Each shadowed alcove held the promise of revelation and redemption, yet also the looming threat of eternal damnation.

Through the corridors of Upton Manor he wandered, a lost soul in search of absolution, his heart heavy with the burden of his wrong doings. And as the darkness closed in around him, he knew that only by confronting the demons of his past could he hope to find the salvation he so desperately sought.

In the vibrant tapestry of his youth, before the sacred vows of priesthood bound him to a life of devotion, Gabriel Gifford stood as a towering figure of ambition and desire. His heart, once aflame with dreams of worldly success and power, propelled him down a treacherous path fraught with temptation and moral compromise, where shadows danced with whispers of forbidden promises.

Born and raised in the idyllic embrace of a quaint village nestled near Brixham, Gabriel and his closest friend, Sam Bellamy, shared a bond forged in the fires of childhood innocence. Beneath the sprawling boughs of ancient oak trees, they whispered secrets and spun dreams, their laughter echoing through the verdant glades like music from a forgotten age. But as the tender years melted into the harsh embrace of adulthood, Gabriel's insatiable hunger for greatness cast a dark cloud over their once unbreakable bond.

It was in the crucible of ambition that he committed one of his most grievous sins, a betrayal that stained his soul with the ink of remorse and regret. Like a serpent coiled in the shadows, envy and greed slithered into his heart, poisoning the wellspring of friendship that had sustained him through the trials of youth. In a moment of weakness, he turned his back on Sam, weaving a tapestry of deceit and manipulation to further his own selfish desires, heedless of the devastation wrought upon his erstwhile companion.

The echoes of his betrayal reverberated through the corridors of time, a haunting melody of shattered trust and fractured bonds. Though the passage of years may have dulled the sharp edges of memory, the spectre of his transgression lingered like a shadow upon his conscience, a reminder of the price paid for the pursuit of earthly glory.

As he stood amidst the crumbling ruins of his past, haunted by the ghost of his former self, he knew that redemption lay beyond the horizon, obscured by the mists of uncertainty. And though the road to absolution may be fraught with peril and penance, he vowed to embark upon the journey with unwavering resolve, seeking forgiveness for sins that weighed heavy upon his soul.

Another dark and tormented chapter in the annals of his tumultuous past unfolded amidst the clandestine whispers of forbidden love, a tempestuous affair that cast a pall of scandal over his once pure soul. The object of his affections bore the name Amelia, a siren whose beguiling allure ensnared his heart in a web of passion and desire, leading him astray from the sacred path ordained by his faith.

Despite the solemn vows of celibacy that bound him to the service of God, he succumbed to the intoxicating embrace of Amelia, their clandestine rendezvous shrouded in the cloak of night, their whispered promises mingling with the sighing winds that whispered through the ancient corridors of his conscience. With each stolen moment, he ventured further into the forbidden depths of their liaison, heedless of the chasm of betrayal yawning wide before him.

The consequences of his illicit dalliance reverberated like thunderclaps through the hallowed halls of his parish, shattering the trust of his flock and tarnishing the sanctity of his calling. For his wrong doings stood as a stark betrayal of the very teachings he had sworn to uphold, a sacrilege that threatened to rend the fabric of his faith asunder.

But his sins knew no bounds, extending their dark tendrils beyond the realm of forbidden love and into the murky depths of greed and avarice. Like a venomous serpent coiled in the shadows, he exploited his position within the church for personal gain, his hands stained with the blood of embezzled funds intended for the noble cause of charity. With each ill gotten coin squandered on lavish indulgences and opulent luxuries, he further cemented his descent into moral depravity, his soul adrift on a sea of unrepentant sin.

As he stood upon the precipice of damnation, he grappled with the weight of his sins, his heart heavy with the burden of guilt and remorse. Yet, amidst the encroaching darkness, a flicker of hope remained, a slender thread of redemption that beckoned him towards the light of absolution, if only he dared to grasp it before it slipped beyond his reach.

As the heavy burden pressed upon him like a leaden weight, he sought refuge within the ancient confines of Upton Manor, hoping that solitude and penance would serve as the crucible for his redemption. Yet, unbeknownst to him, the malevolent forces that lurked within those walls lay in wait, their twisted conspiracies poised to exploit his vulnerabilities and amplify his torment to unfathomable heights.

Within the corridors, Father Gifford found himself ensnared in a maelstrom of spectral apparitions and whispered accusations, each one a ghostly echo of his past, haunting him with relentless ferocity. With every shadow that flickered in the dim candlelight, he felt the icy grip of guilt tighten around his heart, dragging him further into the abyss of despair.

Haunted by the phantoms of his own making, his descent into madness seemed inevitable, the line between reality and delusion blurring with each passing moment. The malevolent entities within Upton Manor, like puppet masters pulling invisible strings, manipulated his deepest fears and darkest desires, twisting them into grotesque manifestations that danced in the shadows of his tortured mind.

As the darkness closed in around him, swallowing him whole, his anguished cry pierced the silence of the night, reverberating off the ancient stones of Upton Manor.

"Why won't you leave me be?" he pleaded, his voice a desperate plea for reprieve from the relentless torment that gnawed at his soul.

But in the oppressive stillness that followed, only the mocking laughter of the malevolent entities answered his call, their sinister whispers echoing through the empty halls like a cruel mockery of his shattered faith.

In the silence that followed, a voice, soft yet unmistakably chilling, slithered into his mind. "You cannot escape us, Gabriel. We are everywhere."

He recoiled, his heart pounding in his chest. "Who are you? What do you want from me?"

"We are the spirits of this manor, Gabriel. We have witnessed your sins, and now you must pay the price," the voice whispered, sending shivers down his spine.

"No... I won't let you control me," he muttered, his voice trembling with defiance.

But the entities within the manor had already sunk their claws into his soul, twisting his thoughts and driving him to madness. In a moment of madness, consumed by the darkness that surrounded him, Father Gifford's mind snapped.

With a gut-wrenching wail, his world collapsed in on itself. His fingers, once tender and loving, now curled into claws of desperation around the delicate throat of his beloved wife, Isabella. Her gasps for air were drowned out by the cacophony of his own anguish, his heart pounding in sync with the frenzied tempo of his actions.

"Forgive me, Isabella," he choked out, his voice a broken whisper amidst the chaos of their shared agony. Tears mingled with the sweat on his brow as he beheld the horror reflected in her wide, terrified eyes. Each strained breath she took felt like a shard of glass piercing his already shattered soul.

But even as he felt her life slipping through his trembling grasp, he couldn't silence the relentless whispers that clawed at the fringes of his sanity. They taunted him with accusations, reminding him of every mistake, every flaw, every moment of weakness that led to this unfathomable tragedy.

In a desperate bid to escape the suffocating weight of his guilt, he tore himself away from Isabella's lifeless form, his chest heaving with the weight of his sorrow. With each step he took, the shadows seemed to close in around him, echoing the torment of his fractured mind.

Fleeing from the once familiar confines of their grand manor, he stumbled blindly into the twilight, his footsteps echoing in the empty corridors of his mind. The fading moon cast an eerie glow upon his anguished figure as he vanished into the darkness, consumed by the relentless storm of his own remorse.

As he stood at the precipice of the nearby cliffs, the tumultuous wind tugged at his hair like the icy fingers of fate. His heart heavy with grief and despair, he gazed out at the churning sea below, its dark waters mirroring the turmoil within him.

A broken sob escaped his lips, echoing against the rugged cliffs as he grappled with the unbearable weight of his sorrow. Each breath felt like a struggle, each moment an eternity of torment. In the depths of his anguish, he made a fateful decision.

With a final, anguished cry torn from the depths of his soul, he surrendered to gravity's embrace, hurtling into the yawning abyss below. The roaring wind swallowed his cry, blending it seamlessly with the crashing waves that awaited him.

As his body plummeted, time seemed to slow, his mind flooded with fragmented memories of happier days now lost to him forever. And then, with a sickening thud, his broken form collided with the jagged rocks below, the impact shattering both flesh and spirit.

Above, in the looming shadows of Upton Manor, unseen eyes watched with an insatiable hunger for retribution. For too long had they suffered in silence, nursing ancient grievances and nursing their thirst for vengeance. Now, as they beheld the shattered remnants of their tormentor far below, a sinister satisfaction twisted their ethereal forms.

Their whispers of malice carried on the wind, mingling with the mournful cries of sea birds circling overhead. In that moment, amidst the desolation and despair, the entities of Upton Manor found a perverse solace, their thirst for retribution at last quenched in the crimson tide washing against the unforgiving cliffs.

As the sun started its ascent in the sky, casting its warm glow over the sprawling grounds of Upton Manor, the ancient stones seemed to whisper secrets of their own. The winds whispered through the trees, carrying with them the echoes of the tragedies that had unfolded within the manor's walls.

Inside the grand halls, the shadows danced in silent lament, their mournful sway a testament to the sorrow that lingered in every corner. But amidst the darkness, a flicker of life remained, a spark of possibility waiting to be ignited.

In the present day, a new chapter was about to unfold in the story of Upton Manor. Perhaps a curious traveller would stumble upon its hidden depths, drawn by tales of its haunted past. Or maybe a brave soul would dare to venture inside, determined to unravel the mysteries that lay within.

Whatever the future held, one thing was certain: the legacy of Father Gifford and the tormented souls who had come before him would continue to echo through the halls of Upton Manor, their stories waiting to be discovered by those brave enough to seek them out.

2

Overwhelmed by a sense of despair, the man stood outside the railway station, mulling over his options as his eyes wandered across the empty street. Without warning, they locked onto a lone vehicle on the opposite end. The strange black car, looked suspiciously like a taxi. He felt a release valve go off in his body as his feet lifted from the pavement and carried him down the street, desperate to reach it before the driver took off. When he got to within a few feet of it, the engine revved as if it were a tiger yawning from a long nap. He put all his strength into his legs, determined to catch it.

"Hey," he shouted, waving his hand wildly.

The car had started up and began moving, but the person behind the wheel paused as he approached. Bending over slightly, the man cautiously rapped his knuckles on the window. The driver's window slowly rolled down, revealing a man in his forties.

"Taxi?" the driver inquired.

"Hello there," he said, taking short gasps of air. "Are you a Uber by any chance? I've been trying to find a ride for a while."

"No, I'm not a Uber," the taxi driver chuckled. "This is my cab though."

He looked at the driver's face,which was weathered and adorned in round glasses - Harry Potter style – with salt and pepper hair and a hint of a paunch hidden beneath a striped button down shirt. He had what people would call "kind eyes" - dark pools of brown, inviting you to take a seat and open your heart up. However, the man looking back at him was ambiguous at best. At first glance he looked white, perhaps Eastern European. But the longer he gazed, the more uncertain he became. His big, bushy moustache twitched, hiding a smile, and that's when he realized he had been staring at the cab driver for a full minute in silence.

He jumped.

"Sorry. Are you taking passengers by any chance? I really need a ride," he asked.

"Yes, of course," the driver replied.

"I need to get to Brixham," the man said, as he hopped into the cab. "It's Higher Brixham, on the road to Kingswear. The place is Upton Manor."

"That'll be up in Cow Town," the driver said.

"That's right," the man replied. "So you know the area?"

He glanced around his new environment. The inside of the cab was spotless, pristine even; not a hint of dust below his feet, and the black leather seats smelled freshly cleaned. The dashboard was another story. It was the only area of the vehicle that could be called cluttered, messy even. He observed the objects that took up the space. A box of Kleenex. A smattering of glitter mingled with the dust – from where? A pewter figurine in the shape of a bull, with two ruby-red gems where the eyes should be. A tiny, black and white photograph, showing two smiling people with their arms around each other.

He squinted, trying to make out the silhouettes, and that's when the driver cleared his throat.

"Should know the area," he replied. "Been a taxi driver here for the past two decades."

The man jumped. "Huh?"

The driver's sparkling eyes looked at him through the rear view mirror.

"Twenty years, friend. Two decades. That's how long I've been driving a cab."

He nodded his head slowly, the rhythmic motion mirroring the gentle pause of his cab as it halted for two figures crossing the street. A woman, her grip firm yet tender around the hand of a toddler, offered a wave of apology as she hurried past. His response was a subtle inclination of his head accompanied by a warm smile, his eyes lingering on the scene with a softness that belied the bustling scene around them.

Beside the mother and child, a tableau unfolded on a nearby bench. Two young women, their passion palpable in the fervour of their embrace, seemed oblivious to the world around them. Their lips met with an intensity that spoke of longing and rebellion, drawing the gaze of an older woman nearby. With a mixture of disapproval and resigned amusement, she shook her head, a silent commentary on the fleeting nature of youth.

Meanwhile, a lone figure sauntered down the roadside, a portable speaker hoisted triumphantly above his head. The music, a cacophony of beats and lyrics, spilled into the street, creating an impromptu soundtrack for the neighbourhood. Despite the volume, his presence was met with nods of recognition and perhaps a hint of admiration from those who knew him. He was a fixture of the community, his eccentricities embraced rather than shunned.

Through the cab's window, the driver observed these vignettes of life, each one a glimpse into the tapestry of humanity that defined the streets of Brixham. In these brief moments, amidst the chaos and cacophony, there existed a quiet beauty — a reminder that amidst the hustle and bustle, moments of connection and authenticity could still be found.

With a gentle press of the accelerator, the cab resumed its journey, carrying its lone occupant towards his destination. And as the scenery shifted and changed outside his window, the driver couldn't help but wonder at the myriad lives intersecting and diverging in the dance of existence.

"So, what are you doing in Brixham?" the driver asked.

"It was time for me to come back," the man answered. "Twenty years in Scotland is a long time to be away from home."

"Is this the first time you've been back since you left?" the driver asked again.

"Yes," he replied.

"That's a long time away mate," he said, letting out a sigh. "Mind you not a lot has changed here."

The traffic lights changed to green and the taxi turned right into Bolton Street.

"Didn't that pub on the corner used to be called the Bolton?" the man asked, pointing out of the window.

"That's right," the driver replied. "They changed the name to the Birdcage a couple of years ago. Do you remember the landlady that ran the old place?"

"Yes, I do," he replied. "I remember her being an alcoholic."

"Smack on," the driver said. "Drank herself to death, you know. She got so pissed one night, she went walking along the Strand and fell into the harbour."

"So she drowned then?" the man asked.

"No," he replied. "The tide was out and she fell onto some rocks and cracked her skull. Not long after, the brewery closed the place down, renovated it, and gave it a new name. It's completely different inside. They say her ghost haunts the place but then again there's lots of ghostly goings on in this area so it wouldn't surprise me. The place you're going to is supposed to be haunted, that old Upton Manor. What brings you going there?"

"I lived there before I moved to Scotland," the man replied. "So it's going to be interesting to move back."

The taxi driver's mouth opened wide.

"So have you bought the place?" he asked, lines forming between his eyebrows.

"What do you mean bought the place?" the man asked.

"Well," the taxi driver replied. "There's been a for sale sign outside the place for years."

"A for sale sign?" the man growled. "The place isn't for sale. It belongs to me."

"I'm just telling you what I know," said the taxi driver. "It seems nobody wants to buy it because it's evil."

The man's jaw tightened. His eyes flashed heat waves at the driver.

"How can anybody buy it when it belongs to me?" the words emptying from his mouth. "Can't you get it into your head that it isn't up for sale?"

The final hiss in his voice warned the driver about his feelings.

The tyres crunched on the gravel as the cab pulled into the driveway.

"Here we are. Here's the entrance to the old manor," he said. "I 'll have to leave you here because I'm not going any further inside that place."

"As you wish," the man said, and got out of the taxi.

To the right, opposite a red postbox, were two stone pillars, partially covered in ivy. The rusted wrought iron gates were open. Below the large Boyce 'For Sale' board, fixed to the left hand gatepost, was a smaller, barely legible sign which had Upton printed on it. Then another similar sign on the right hand gatepost had Manor printed on it.

The man turned round to pay his fare but the taxi and driver had disappeared.

The wet gravel squelched as he made his way up the drive. The low, black metal fence, glistening as if they had just been painted, revealed views towards the Breakwater and across the bay. After about a quarter of a mile, the drive curved sharply to the right and he walked across a cattle grid. Just then, the building came into view.

The decaying structure loomed before him, its once grand façade now a testament to the ravages of time. Like a tired old man leaning precariously to one side, it seemed to peer at him through cracked windows, its weather-beaten walls whispering long forgotten tales to anyone who cared to listen. As he stood before it, a pang of sorrow gripped his heart, tears welling up in his eyes at the sight of its dilapidated state.

Once, this had been a stately manor, a beacon of elegance and grandeur nestled amidst the rolling hillside. But now, it stood forgotten, a shadow of its former self, hidden away from the world by overgrown foliage and neglect.

Despite its once proud history, no one spared it a second glance. It was a relic of the past, relegated to obscurity by the relentless march of progress. Yet, for him, it held a special significance. Memories flooded his mind as he gazed upon its crumbling state. He remembered the laughter that had once echoed through its halls, the warmth of family gatherings, and the sense of belonging that had filled every corner of the estate. Now, all that remained were faded echoes and the haunting whispers of bygone days.

Why did no one notice it, he wondered? Perhaps it was the distance from the road, or the air of mystery that surrounded it, shrouding it in an aura of forgotten secrets. Or maybe, in their relentless pursuit of "important" matters, people simply chose to overlook what lay beyond the beaten path.

But to him, this place held a treasure trove of memories, a connection to a past that refused to be erased by the passage of time. And as he stood there, his gaze lingering on the crumbling edifice before him, he realized that some things were worth venturing into the unknown for — even if the rest of the world deemed them unworthy of attention.

He didn't see it as old or unfixable but saw the potential to be a unique and beautiful home once again. As he stood, eyes penetrating it, he shivered, as though ice had replaced his spine. It stood silently still and he could see that it was losing part of its skin, producing tiny, white flakes arranged around the forecourt, and the shingles on top of the roof were trying to hang on as best they could. The central part was fronted by a classically proportioned Tudor façade clad in weather-stained white rendering, on three floors, or four if the cellar was included. On either side were tall sash windows and there were two dormer windows in the slate tiled roof. Vines formed a twisted web upon the side of it, reaching their tentacles towards the roof.

And so, with determination coursing through his veins, he took a tentative step forward, his resolve unshakeable. For in that moment, he knew that he carried with him the weight of history, and it was his duty to ensure that it was not forgotten.

He was surprised to see the door slightly ajar and as he placed his hand on it, it begrudgingly creaked open with a resounding echo that seemed to fill the place. A musty, dank odour teased his nose. Cobwebs once attached flowed freely in the air as the open door brought light to a well worn floor. The light gave notice to the peeling paint on the walls. The new air gave life to a stuffiness that entrapped the hallway. If it hadn't been for the intermittent creaks and moans he would have sworn he'd gone deaf.

Without making a sound, he entered the dark living room. The windows hadn't seen a dusting cloth in years, which made the shadows that roamed around the room much more conspicuous. Faded and torn white sheets covered the overturned sofa and chairs now drowning in dust and revealing deep grooves on the ground where they used to be. Picture frames hanging askew on the walls made him feel giddy. Choosing the right book from the misplaced grand bookcase in the corner of the room, undisturbed for a long time, could reveal a secret doorway into another world. He made his way back into the hallway.

A shimmer of light came from behind a door. He approached and opened it. He had reached the bathroom. The single window was mildly dirty, a flood of light flowed into the room. Dust swirled around as he made his way inside. The medicine cabinet mirror lay shattered in pieces on the floor tiles. An empty medicine bottle lay in the porcelain sink. The only sound to be heard was the dripping of the tap. A closer look revealed the discolouration of the water, a brownish concoction. A lone mouse scurried at the bottom of the tub. Never having a visitor in a while, it curiously eyed him up before scuttling away.

He didn't seem to be making much progress as he headed towards the staircase. As he moved nearer, it appeared to move further away from him. "I don't think it wants me to get near it," he thought.

Eventually, he and the staircase met.Standing at the foot of it, he peered upwards, a shiver coursing through his spine. His imagination ran wild, conjuring images of a headless phantom lurking in the darkness above, waiting to pounce and send him into the depths of terror. With a hesitant breath, he began his ascent, each step a precarious journey into the unknown.

The staircase protested with every movement, its timbers straining against the weight of years gone by. The air was thick with anticipation, as if the very walls themselves held their breath, waiting for some unseen horror to unfold. His footsteps sounded deafeningly loud in the oppressive silence, each creak and groan of the stairs echoing through the empty place.

With each step, the tension mounted, his pulse quickening with every beat. It felt as though the entire manor was holding its breath, as if any moment could be its last before the stairs crumbled beneath him. Yet still, he pressed on, driven by a mixture of fear and determination.

At last, he reached the top landing, a sense of relief washing over him like a wave. But his respite was short lived as he turned to the right, his final destination looming ominously before him. The door stood defiantly closed, as if daring him to enter its forbidden domain.

Summoning his courage, he approached it, his hand trembling as he reached out to grasp the cold brass knob. With a tentative push, he attempted to open it, but the door refused to yield, as if held fast by some unseen force. With a grunt of effort, he shoved against the stubborn barrier, the muscles in his arms straining against the resistance. Slowly, inch by inch, it began to give way, the sound of wood scraping against wood filling the air like a sinister symphony.

Finally, with one last mighty push, it swung open, revealing the room beyond. But what he saw made his blood run cold.

A dresser had been pushed against the door from within, as if to barricade it shut and prevent anyone from entering. It stood as a silent sentinel, its wooden frame weathered and worn with age, yet still solid and unyielding in its purpose.

For a moment, he hesitated, the hairs on the back of his neck standing on end as a chill ran down his spine. But then, with a determined step forward, he crossed the threshold into the darkness beyond, steeling himself for whatever horrors awaited him within.

The dim moonlight seeped through the window, casting eerie shadows across the room. He stepped cautiously into the darkness, his eyes adjusting to the faint outlines of furniture. There, amidst the gloom, he could discern the silhouette of a bed, its shape hauntingly familiar.

Curiosity tugged at him, pulling him closer to the bedstead. As he drew nearer, details emerged—a toy soldier, its once proud stature now diminished by the absence of its head, lay abandoned on the coverlet. Memories flooded his mind, of days long gone when he and his twin brother would wage epic battles with similar toys, their laughter echoing through the manor.

Outside, the wind moaned mournfully, its lament mingling with the rustle of leaves and the creak of branches. The symphony of nature seemed to swell in intensity, as if echoing the turmoil within.

In the far corner, a diminutive chair swayed gently, its movements unsettlingly rhythmic. Was it a trick of the shadows, or was there something more sinister at play?

Without warning, a primal howl pierced the air, reverberating through the very walls. His heart quickened, a shiver coursing down his spine as he instinctively reached for the door, eager to escape the encroaching darkness. With a trembling hand, he pushed the door shut, its ominous creak drowned out by the cacophony outside. Yet, as he turned to leave, a chill gripped him—a sensation of unseen eyes upon him.

And then, in the suffocating silence that followed, he turned slowly, only to be confronted by a sight that froze the blood in his veins—a spectral figure, its form barely discernible in the dim light, looming just beyond the threshold.

A silent scream clawed its way up his throat, trapped within the confines of his terror stricken mind. For in that fleeting moment, he knew—he was not alone.

"Good evening, Doctor Kendal," the voice said. "Welcome home."

The man stared in disbelief at the woman standing before him. She was dressed in a vintage gown that seemed to belong to a bygone era, her dark hair cascading down in loose waves. Her eyes, a shade of deep emerald, held a mysterious glint. As the door behind her creaked open, a dim light illuminated the room, revealing a haunting beauty that seemed out of place in the decaying surroundings.

"Who are you?" he stammered, his voice barely audible.

"I am the caretaker," she replied, her voice carrying a soft yet commanding tone. "I have been waiting for your return."

He felt a shiver run down his spine.

"Waiting for me? How do you know me?" he asked.

She moved closer, her gown rustling with an ethereal grace.

"I have watched over Upton Manor for centuries. It is your bloodline that binds you to this place."

"My bloodline?" he repeated, his confusion deepening.

"Yes," she continued. "You are the descendant of the original owner, and the manor recognizes its rightful heir."

The man struggled to comprehend the surreal encounter.

"But why now? Why after all these years?" he asked.

"Upton Manor is awakening," she explained. "It senses a darkness encroaching upon it, and only the true heir can unlock its secrets and restore its former glory."

He glanced around the dilapidated room, trying to reconcile the mystical tale with the stark reality.

"What secrets does this place hold?" he asked.

Her eyes glowed brighter as she spoke, "Hidden passages, forgotten chambers, and a history entwined with both light and shadow. The manor yearns to reveal its stories to you."

As she spoke, the atmosphere in the room shifted. The air seemed charged with an otherworldly energy. She extended her hand towards a seemingly ordinary wall, and to the man's amazement, a hidden door materialized.

"Go, explore the depths of Upton Manor," she urged. "Discover the legacy that awaits you, and embrace the destiny that binds you to this place."

With a mix of trepidation and curiosity, he stepped through the hidden doorway, leaving behind the desolate bedroom. The air in the passage was cool, and a soft glow emanated from ancient candle holders lining the walls. The manor seemed to come alive with a whispered promise of revelations and mysteries.

As he ventured deeper into the hidden recesses, he realized that his return had set in motion a chain of events that transcended time itself. Upton Manor, with its secrets and echoes of the past, awaited the awakening of its true heir.

3

Seasoned author Ben Sanders stood at the precipice of uncertainty in his illustrious career. The once steady stream of ideas had dwindled to a mere trickle, leaving him adrift in a sea of creative stagnation. The ever expanding void between projects had stretched beyond the realm of anticipation, gnawing at his confidence and leaving him grappling with a profound drought of inspiration. The well that once brimmed with creativity had seemingly run dry, and he found himself standing at a crossroads, unsure of the path that lay ahead.

It was in this poignant moment of professional limbo that a peculiar invitation disrupted the stillness of his writing sanctuary. The envelope, weathered and worn, bore an elaborate wax seal bearing an unfamiliar insignia. It lay on his cluttered desk like a riddle demanding unravelling, a beacon of curiosity amidst the chaos of his thoughts. With trembling hands, he delicately broke the seal, revealing an impeccably handwritten letter that would alter the trajectory of his creative journey.

The letter extended a mysterious invitation to Upton Manor, a place shrouded in legend and whispered rumours—a sanctuary for the creative soul. Its rich history and secluded atmosphere promised to be steeped in inspiration and solitude, offering respite from the relentless clamour of the outside world. The words, elegant and alluring, spoke to him in a way that ignited a long dormant spark within him, kindling a glimmer of hope amidst the shadows of doubt that clouded his mind.

The signature at the bottom of the letter simply bore the enigmatic title, "The Caretaker," leaving him to ponder the identity of the mysterious benefactor who had extended this tantalizing offer. With his curiosity piqued and his heart heavy with anticipation, he knew that he could not ignore the call of Upton Manor. It beckoned to him like a distant lighthouse guiding a weary traveller home, offering the promise of renewal and the chance to rediscover the passion that had once fuelled his creativity.

Armed with nothing but his pen and the flickering flame of inspiration that had been reignited within him, Ben set out on a journey into the unknown. Little did he know that his decision to accept the Caretaker's invitation would lead him down a path fraught with mystery, intrigue, and unexpected revelations—a journey that would test his courage, challenge his beliefs, and ultimately reshape the very fabric of his reality.

Despite the ambiguity shrouding the invitation, the allure of Upton Manor proved too potent for him to resist. With a cocktail of excitement and trepidation swirling within him, he began the process of packing his belongings, preparing for a journey into the heart of the English countryside.

As he navigated the winding roads and picturesque landscapes, he couldn't shake the feeling that he was stepping into the unknown. Upton Manor awaited him like a silent guardian, its secrets hidden within the walls, and the promise of inspiration echoing through its corridors.

The journey into the heart of the Devonshire countryside marked the beginning of a new chapter in his life—a chapter that held the potential to rekindle the flames of his creativity or plunge him into the depths of an even greater mystery. Little did he know that Upton Manor held secrets that transcended the boundaries of his imagination, and the enigmatic Caretaker's invitation was just the beginning of a journey that would test the limits of his perception and unravel the threads of reality and fiction.

As twilight draped its muted hues over the quaint fishing village of Brixham, a mist, delicate as gossamer, embraced the time worn edifice known as Upton Manor. The tendrils of ethereal fog caressed the centuries old stone walls, lending an aura of mystery to the grand estate. Within this spectral shroud, a lone figure materialized—a woman, her silhouette framed against the wooden patio furniture, a silent observer of the garden's transformation into an autumnal tapestry.

In the cool embrace of the mist, the woman indulged in languid puffs from a cigarette. Grey wisps of smoke meandered away, entwining with the ethereal tendrils, as if whispering secrets to the ancient oaks that stood sentinel in the garden. The fragrance of the ash clung to the damp air, a subtle, haunting note in the symphony of the approaching night.

Ben, drawn by the allure of nostalgia, approached at a leisurely pace. The woman's attire, a black trouser-and-jacket ensemble paired with a crisp white blouse, exuded a professional air that resonated with the surroundings. As he neared, the scent of his aftershave wrestled against the damp, the olfactory duel preceding their inevitable encounter.

Clad in the ash blond hues of his hair and the light tones of his face, he observed her with discerning eyes of deep, expressive golden-brown. Unfathomable and faraway, those eyes bespoke a uniqueness that transcended the ordinary. His gait, confident yet unhurried, bespoke a presence that demanded attention, though not necessarily the kind that stirred a crowd.

She discarded the cigarette with a nonchalant grace, extinguishing its glow under the heel of her shoe.

As Ben closed the distance, she turned, acknowledging him with eyes that seemed detached, their depths reminiscent of forgotten marbles in the attic of an ancestral mansion—a gaze unyielding, untethered from the present, like death taking a leisurely stroll through the corridors of time.

"Mr. Sanders?" she inquired, extending her hand, a perfunctory formality.

"Please, call me Ben," he replied, the handshake a meeting of two disparate worlds.

"You found the place all right, then?" she continued, her eyes revealing nothing, as if veiled in a mask of indifference.

"Yes, I used to come to Brixham a lot when I was a kid. I lived just down the road. So..." he began, his words trailing into the mist, laden with a sense of familiarity.

"That's nice," she interjected, an interruption that signalled the commencement of a discourse, choreographed with the detachment of a practised routine. "I thought I'd show you around the manor and make sure you're all settled in."

The resonance of their footsteps echoed through the entrance as the lock clicked, sealing them within the hallowed halls of Upton Manor. The air within seemed to thicken with history, each creak of the floorboards narrating tales of bygone eras.

"It's a wonderful place," she commented, her smile painted on like a portrait that failed to bridge the gap between her lips and her eyes. "Dates back to the 16th century and is steeped in history."

"Looks amazing," he remarked, his inquisitive eyes absorbing the intricacies of the centuries old dwelling. The architecture whispered of forgotten stories, secrets entwined in the very fabric of the manor.

The tour unfolded, Mrs. Parkes, guided Ben through the labyrinth of rooms, each a chapter in the annals of the estate's storied past. The heavy oak furniture and ancient tapestries bore witness to the eons, a silent testimony to the passage of time.

Amidst the exploration, a moment of revelation hung in the air, like the subtle scent of aged leather in a library—a truth, delicate yet unspoken. Her hands entwined, approached the precipice of disclosure.

"Now, I need to explain something that's a little embarrassing," she began, the confession drawing Ben into the clandestine folds of the manor's history.

"What's that?" he inquired, a sense of curiosity etched on his face.

"The letter didn't mention it, but there is an annex to the building," she confessed, her words unveiling a hidden facet of Upton Manor. "It's in the eastern wing, actually. It's behind that door over there," she said, pointing to a door in the corner of the room. "Well, there's a small passageway behind the door that leads to the annex. You needn't worry, though; it's always kept locked."

"Why should that be embarrassing?" Ben questioned, his arms folded, a silent challenge for her to unravel the intrigue.

"The thing is, someone lives there," she disclosed, a subtle pause accentuating the weight of her revelation.

"Lives there?" his response bore a hint of irritation, a ripple of unrest in the tranquillity of the manor.

"I'm sorry if it seems to put you off," she admitted, her gaze now avoiding his, as if bracing for the repercussions of her confession.

"I can see why, Mrs. Parkes," he replied, a firm acknowledgement of the unexpected revelation. "I was kind of hoping to have this place to myself, you know?"

"You will have the place to yourself," she reassured, a plea in her voice. "The tenant's an old doctor. His name's Dr. Kendal. You won't even know he's there. He hasn't left the place in years."

The tension between the two lingered, a silent negotiation between the desire for solitude and the presence of an enigmatic occupant. Ben, ever the observer, held his ground, a silent demand for transparency in the midst of veiled disclosures.

"I must be honest with you, Mrs. Parkes. I really think you ought to have mentioned this in the letter, you know?" he asserted, a proclamation that echoed through the hallowed halls of the manor.

"I mean..." she attempted to interject, her words trailing into the unresolved tension.

"No, no, please let me continue," Ben interrupted, his voice gaining intensity. "When I was invited to the place, I didn't expect I'd be sharing it with a complete stranger."

"I'm sorry," she apologized, her words a fragile attempt to mend the frayed threads of understanding. "But I can assure you, Dr. Kendal won't be of any nuisance. He hardly makes a sound. I mean, you've seen the size of this place. You'll have almost the entire manor all to yourself."

The negotiation concluded, a truce forged in the dimly lit corridors. The tour continued, each room a silent witness to the unspoken pact between tenant and host. Yet, the looming presence of Dr. Kendal cast a shadow on the anticipated solitude of Ben's sojourn.

"Don't you think I should introduce myself?" Ben insisted, a plea for a semblance of familiarity with the occupant who shared the ancient walls.

"Oh, I doubt he'd answer the door," she responded, her words a gentle plea for acceptance. "He likes to keep himself to himself. Shall we go downstairs?"

"Yes, of course," he acquiesced, the allure of the manor overshadowed by the cryptic presence of its elusive tenant.

"You'll be fine," she assured him as they stepped outside, keys in hand. The night unfolded around them, a tapestry of stars adorning the inky canvas of the sky. "Here are the keys to the front door and back door. You have my telephone number, don't you?"

"Yes," he confirmed, the metallic jingle of keys in his palm signalling the commencement of his solitary tenure.

"Do feel free to call me if there's anything else you need," she offered, her words a lifeline extended to bridge the gap between uncertainty and reassurance.

"Thanks. I'm sure I'll be fine," he replied, the words a ritualistic exchange, a promise whispered into the night.

"Okay, when you leave, just put the keys in the letterbox at the end of the drive, and I'll pop by and pick them up," she instructed, the practicalities of the arrangement grounding their ethereal journey within the manor.

"Will do," he agreed, the keys now bearing the weight of responsibility, a symbolic commitment to the silent pact forged within the walls of Upton Manor.

"Enjoy your stay," she concluded, her words hanging in the air like a benediction, as if invoking the ancient spirits that lingered within the heart of the estate.

As the heavy oak door closed behind her, Ben found himself standing alone in the grandeur of Upton Manor. His eyes, cast downward, met the intricate patterns of the ancient carpet beneath him. The mist outside seemed to seep through the windows, as if seeking entry into the enigmatic narratives that unfolded within the manor's walls.

The journey within was just beginning, a chapter yet to be written in the unfolding saga of Upton Manor. With each step, the echoes of his footfalls resonated through the dimly lit corridors, blending with the whispers of history that clung to the air.

In the living room, he found himself drawn to the heavy oak table that stood as a testament to the bygone eras. His laptop, a modern artefact amidst the antiquity, beckoned him like a portal to uncharted realms. As he opened it, the soft glow of the screen illuminated his face, a solitary figure in the vast expanse of the ancient room.

His fingers hovered over the keys, poised to transcribe the essence of the manor into the written word. Yet, the mysterious Dr. Kendal, concealed behind the locked door, remained an unexplored character in the unfolding narrative.

Leaning back in the antique chair, he pondered the intricacies of solitude and companionship within the hallowed halls of the manor. The ticking of the grandfather clock, a symphony of time, resonated with the steady rhythm of his contemplations.

The creaking floorboards, the whispering wind outside, and the distant hum of a forgotten era formed the backdrop to his musings. Amidst the timeless tapestry of history, he found himself entangled in the enigmatic threads of the manor's legacy.

As his gaze wandered towards the window, the boundaries between the present and the past blurred. The flickering candlelight cast dancing shadows on the walls, as if the spirits of the bygone years whispered secrets to the attentive listener.

The looming presence of the locked door to the annex, where Dr. Kendal resided, became a symbolic threshold—an invitation to explore the hidden corners of the manor. Tossing the keys between his hands, Ben contemplated the choices that awaited him in the corridors of the estate.

With a slow exhale, he rose from the antique chair and approached a painting above the fireplace—a depiction of the manor with a broken cart in front. As his eyes traced the strokes of the artist's brush, a fleeting movement caught his attention.

Beneath a small glass jar on the mantelpiece, a lifeless cockroach lay in repose. Delicately picking it up with his forefinger and thumb, he regarded the insect with a mixture of fascination and irony.

"Ugh. Now there's three of us in this place, Mrs. Parkes," he muttered, his gaze shifting towards the door that led to the annex—a portal to the unknown.

The building, once a silent witness to the ebb and flow of time, now pulsed with the anticipation of untold stories. The dead insect, the locked door, the mysterious Dr. Kendal and the unexplored chapters of Upton Manor hinted at a narrative yet to unfold—a tale that resonated with the whispers of the past and the enigma of the present.

As he stood at the crossroads of solitude and shared occupancy, Ben felt the weight of the manor's history pressing upon him. With a lingering glance at the locked door, he knew that the chapters within the manor were not just written in ink but inscribed in the very essence of its walls.

The steady ticking of the grandfather clock, now a companion in his solitary contemplation, became the metronome for the unwritten symphony of his stay. With the keys clutched in his hand, he embarked on a journey that promised not just solitude but the unravelling of the veiled heritage concealed within the heart of Upton Manor.

The shadows danced on the walls as he stood at the precipice of a conundrum, contemplating the mysteries that lay within the manor's core. The rhythmic ticking of the grandfather clock seemed to synchronize with the beating of his heart, creating an intimate symphony that echoed through the vast expanse of the living room.

Lost in thought, he decided to explore the manor's library, an ancient room adorned with shelves that groaned under the weight of countless volumes. The scent of aged paper and leather enveloped him as he ran his fingers along the spines, each book a potential gateway to forgotten realms.

As he delved into the words of long dead authors and explored the tales of centuries past, the boundaries between fiction and reality blurred. The flickering candlelight cast eerie shadows on the time worn pages, breathing life into characters long confined to the realms of imagination.

The distant hoot of a lone owl echoed through the corridors, a haunting melody that seemed to resonate with the secrets locked within Upton Manor's walls. He couldn't shake the feeling that the very essence of the manor was alive, pulsating with stories waiting to be unravelled.

In the midst of his literary exploration, a peculiar tome caught his attention—a dusty leather-bound book tucked away in the corner of a forgotten shelf. Its spine cracked as he gingerly opened it, revealing pages filled with cryptic symbols and handwritten notes. A shiver ran down his spine as he realized this was no ordinary book; it was a journal chronicling the enigmatic history of Upton Manor.

Words penned by long lost caretakers and eccentric inhabitants hinted at supernatural occurrences, hidden passages, and the mysterious presence of Dr. Kendal. The more Ben read, the more he felt entangled in a web of secrets that transcended the boundaries of reality.

With each revelation, the weight of the manor's history bore down on him. The echoes of past footsteps and whispers of forgotten conversations seemed to replay in the air around him. It was as if the very essence of Upton Manor yearned to share its untold tales with the one who dared to venture into its depths.

Closing the mysterious journal, he decided to retire to his room, the heavy oak door creaking softly behind him. As he ascended the staircase, he couldn't escape the feeling that unseen eyes followed his every move. The portrait lined hallways seemed to come alive with the watchful gazes of long gone residents, their stories lingering in the air like echoes of an ancient symphony.

Reaching his room, Ben found himself once again at the crossroads of curiosity and caution. The flickering candle on his bedside table cast dancing shadows on the four poster bed, a silent invitation to unravel the mysteries that awaited him in the heart of Upton Manor.

With the ancient journal clutched in his hand and the enigmatic door to the annex looming in his thoughts, Ben knew that the night held more than just solitude. It held the promise of an extraordinary journey, where the lines between reality and the supernatural would blur, and the tales of Upton Manor would weave themselves into the fabric of his own existence.

As he extinguished the candle's flame, plunging the room into darkness, a quiet whisper seemed to linger in the air—a whisper that beckoned him to explore the shadows, unlock the secrets, and embrace the unfolding saga that awaited him in the heart of the ancient estate.

And so, in the stillness of Upton Manor's night, Ben surrendered himself to the unknown, ready to embark on a journey that would redefine not only his understanding of creativity but also the very essence of his existence.

37

4

The sun waged a futile battle against the thick, looming clouds, casting an eerie and surreal light over the harbour as Ben leisurely strolled into town. The atmosphere was chilled, prompting the tourists to abandon their typical T-shirts and shorts for layers of warmth, creating a captivating scene of bundled figures against the grey backdrop.

Brixham, a town steeped in memories that reverberated with the joyous laughter of teenage escapades, had undergone a profound transformation since Ben's previous visit. Where once its streets had been alive with the vibrant energy of youth, now lay a nostalgic landscape tinged with the bitter sweet echoes of bygone days. Three bustling amusement arcades, once the cherished playgrounds of Ben and his comrades, had dwindled to a solitary survivor, standing as a solemn sentinel amidst the passage of time.

As he wandered the familiar streets, he couldn't help but feel a pang of melancholy at the sight of the solitary arcade, its neon lights flickering with a muted glow that seemed to mirror the fading memories of his youth. Gone were the carefree days of endless summers spent chasing thrills and laughter, replaced now by the sombre realization that time had inexorably moved forward, leaving behind only traces of what once was.

Yet, amidst the wistful nostalgia that hung heavy in the air, there lingered a faint glimmer of hope – a reminder that while the past may be but a distant memory, the spirit of youth and adventure still danced in the hearts of those willing to embrace the journey ahead. And so, with a wistful smile and a heart heavy with reminiscence, he pressed forward, ready to discover what new adventures awaited him in the ever evolving tapestry of life.

As the imminent bank holiday weekend loomed, a few lingering holidaymakers wandered around in the arcade. Amidst them, a frustrated young man struggled with a claw-like contraption, attempting to seize a cuddly toy from a glass cabinet. Chuckling to himself, Ben watched the comical scene unfold, a silent observer in the evolving tapestry of the town.

Next to him, three schoolgirls hesitated at a coin operated machine. Seizing the moment, Ben inserted a 10p coin, contemplating whether to release it into the game. The coin joined the others, stacking up without triggering the elusive reward below.

As the tantalizing scent of sizzling hot dogs danced on the breeze, it was as if the very aroma reached out to ensnare his senses, tempting him with the promise of indulgence. He couldn't help but be drawn to the guilty pleasure that awaited, a craving that stirred within him despite the nagging awareness of its less than healthy allure.

With a wry smile playing on his lips, he succumbed to the irresistible temptation, knowing full well the consequences of his culinary weakness. The thought of greasy frankfurters nestled snugly within undersized rolls brought both a twinge of guilt and a surge of anticipation, a guilty pleasure that beckoned him like an old friend.

As he placed his order, the familiar hiss of the grill and the clang of metal spatulas filled the air, adding to the ambiance of indulgence that surrounded him. And when a cold Coke was offered as the perfect accompaniment, he accepted without hesitation, recognizing the ritualistic pairing as a time honoured tradition meant to elevate the entire experience to new heights.

With his mouth watering in anticipation, he eagerly awaited the arrival of his meal, knowing that in that moment of blissful indulgence, the worries of the world would fade away, if only for a brief moment. For sometimes, amidst the chaos of life, there was solace to be found in the simple pleasure of a perfectly grilled hot dog and an ice cold Coke, a reminder that even the smallest moments of indulgence could bring a sense of joy and contentment that transcended the ordinary.

The majestic silhouette of the Golden Hind loomed large against the backdrop of the harbour, its weathered hull a testament to tales of maritime history and adventure. As he meandered along the promenade, his gaze drawn inexorably toward the iconic vessel, he couldn't help but feel a sense of awe at its enduring presence.

With each step he took, the salty tang of the sea mingled with the crisp breeze, invigorating his senses and infusing him with a renewed appreciation for the maritime heritage that permeated every corner of the harbour. From the creaking of rigging to the distant calls of seagulls wheeling overhead, every sound seemed to harmonize with the rhythmic ebb and flow of the tides, creating a symphony of sights and sounds that stirred the soul.

Before he knew it, he found himself standing at the edge of the breakwater, the granite structure stretching out before him like a sentinel guarding the entrance to the harbour. With the waves crashing against the rocks below and the seagulls wheeling overhead, he felt a profound sense of connection to the sea – a reminder of the timeless bond between mankind and the ever changing tides of destiny.

As he stood there, lost in reverie, Ben couldn't help but marvel at the beauty and complexity of the world around him. In that moment, surrounded by the salty embrace of the sea and the rich tapestry of maritime history that surrounded him, he felt truly alive, a small but integral part of something much greater than himself.

"I'll take a nice stroll to the end and back," he thought, envisioning savouring his hot dog and Coke along the way. But there was a formidable obstacle to overcome first – the resident seagulls.

The absence of many people in this part of town left him virtually alone, immersed in the symphony of the sea. The rocks, resembling indented slabs of black marble, gleamed with the afterglow of the high tide. Just as he was about to relish a bite of his hot dog, the harmonious ambiance shattered.

Squawking and quarrelling sounds reached his ears, and soon the seagulls came into view. The unmistakable noise revealed their intent – the hot dog clutched in his hand was their coveted prize.

They initially approached with a grace that belied their impending attack. The first one, with a cannibalistic glint in its eye, locked onto Ben as its victim. Tucking its wings, the gull swooped down like an avenging angel of death.

"What the fuck's going on!" he yelled, bracing himself for the impending onslaught. The seagulls screamed and circled, screeching and plummeting just above his head. In a swift concession, he ran towards the end of the Breakwater, pursued by the angry horde. Their fishy breath accompanied their dive-bombing tactics.

Finally admitting defeat, he could smell the mouthwatering blend of mustard and ketchup in the hot dog as he violently tossed it into the air. The gulls, in a frenzy, attacked the airborne treat, ensuring it never reached the ground before disappearing down their greedy gullets.

As the waves crashed along the Breakwater, the cacophonous marauders receded into the distance, searching for their next victim. The tang of salt lingered in the air as Ben turned around, heading back toward the shoreline. A lone seagull stood before him, beak raised to the sky, triumphantly squawking while the hot dog wrapper floated gently down.

From the Breakwater, he gazed across at Brixham, its higgledy-piggledy brightly painted houses reminiscent of a waiting jigsaw puzzle yearning to be completed. With the adrenaline of the seagull encounter subsiding and stress weighing heavily, he decided to retreat to the manor along the coastal path via St. Mary's Bay.

The solitary walk offered him an opportunity for introspection. While traversing the quiet path, he contemplated the content for his book. Something in the tranquillity of the environment had sparked inspiration, be it the crisp freshness or the calming sea air. Everything seemed suspended in a moment of stillness and quietude, allowing him to attune to the sounds of insects and the distant sea.

The enticing aroma of freshly brewed tea wafted through the air, guiding him toward the welcoming embrace of the Berry Head Hotel. Drawn by the promise of warmth and comfort, he couldn't resist the urge to pause and indulge in the simple pleasure of a steaming cup.

Entering the cosy confines of the hotel's tearoom, he was enveloped in a sense of tranquillity, the gentle hum of conversation and clinking of china providing a soothing backdrop to his thoughts. With each sip of the piping hot tea, he felt a wave of revitalization wash over him, as if the very essence of the brew infused him with renewed vigour and purpose.

Gazing out across the panoramic vista of the bay, he felt a sense of awe wash over him, the overcast weather lending an air of mystery and enchantment to the scene before him. Despite the grey skies above, there was a quiet beauty to be found in the rugged coastline and the gentle sway of boats bobbing in the marina, a reminder of the timeless allure of the sea.

Lost in the moment, he allowed himself to fully savour the experience, allowing the rich flavours of the tea to mingle with the bracing sea air and the tranquil ambiance of his surroundings. In that fleeting moment of bliss, he found himself infused with a sense of clarity and purpose, ready to continue his journey back to the manor with a renewed sense of energy and determination.

Continuing his leisurely stroll, Ben found himself enveloped in a serenity unlike any other as he ambled past St. Mary's Bay. The symphony of nature's melodies, from the rhythmic crashing of waves against the rugged shore to the gentle rustle of leaves in the breeze, invoked a flood of nostalgic memories of carefree days spent frolicking on the sun kissed sands of his youth.

As he reluctantly tore his gaze away from the captivating seascape, he noticed how the recent drizzle had bestowed a new-found freshness upon the quaint town. Each droplet clinging to the verdant foliage overhead seemed to refract the soft light, casting a celestial glow that bathed the surroundings in an ethereal ambiance, as if nature itself were putting on a show of divine beauty.

Lost in this reverie, Ben's footsteps carried him effortlessly back to the manor that stood as a sentinel against the backdrop of the rolling countryside. Across the meticulously manicured driveway, his attention was drawn to a figure amidst the vibrant blooms of the garden. A young woman, her silhouette softened by the misty afternoon light, delicately plucked wild flowers, infusing the air with the sweet scent of nature's bounty.

"Hello," he called, unintentionally startling her. The flowers dropped from her hands.

"Sorry, I didn't mean to frighten you," he apologized.

"I didn't realize anyone had moved in," she remarked, fingers on her chin.

"Oh, no, it's not permanent," he explained, tracing the impression on his finger where his wedding band used to be. "It's just a retreat for a while."

"Ah, nice," she replied.

"Do you like flowers?" he asked, raising his eyebrows, pointing to the scattered blossoms.

"Sorry?" she asked, tilting her head.

"The flowers," he reiterated.

"Oh, yes," she replied. "You don't mind me picking them, do you?"

"Oh, no. No, not at all," he assured her. "Are you a local?"

"Yes," she confirmed. "I live in one of the flats at the back of here. Upton Manor Wing. I'm Annie. Annie Tolcher."

Clearly lost in creative musings, Annie emanated an aura of introspection. Her eyes, the colour of wet earth, spoke volumes of a beautiful soul. Her warm smile, tinged with shyness, and the melodious quality of her voice created an enchanting atmosphere in the chilly air.

"Ben," he introduced himself. "Ben Sanders."

"It's nice to meet you," she greeted.

"Nice to meet you, too," he responded. "If you ever want more, just pick them."

"Maybe I will," she considered. "Thanks. How long are you here for?"

"I'm here for eight weeks," he answered. "Hey, do you know the old doctor who lives in the annex?"

"What annex?" she inquired, stepping back.

"The annex off my living room," he clarified.

"That's weird," Annie commented. "The only place I thought was behind the manor are the flats at the back where I live. The building used to be the servants' quarters who worked at the manor but was sold as a separate building some years ago and was converted to flats."

"What, you never heard that a doctor lived here?" he pressed.

"Actually," she admitted, "Two doctors used to live here, but I thought it was just an old empty place now."

"Yes, me, too," he acknowledged. "But apparently, the annex has a permanent resident."

"I told you there's no annex," she insisted, shaking her head. "There's only Upton Manor Wing attached to this place. If you get a ladder and look over the wall, you'll see for yourself. Maybe it's another room attached to your living room. Do you talk to him?"

"Nope," he confessed. "The door's locked. He never comes out. And no one comes to see him, either."

"That's quite sad," she mused, looking at the floor.

"Yes. A bit creepy, to be honest," he admitted.

"Are you scared?" she asked.

"A little," he confessed. "Perhaps I should grow a pair."

"I suppose this place can get a bit creepy if you're alone all the time," she empathized. "How come you didn't come with a friend or a girlfriend?"

"Well, I don't have a girlfriend," he disclosed. "And I suppose this self-imposed isolation sort of comes with the territory."

"What territory?" she inquired.

"I'm a writer," Ben revealed.

"Oh, really?" Annie's face lit up.

"Yes," he confirmed. "Well, I say I'm a writer, but I'm struggling to string a sentence together at the minute."

"Got a bit of writer's block going on?" she guessed.

"You know," he admitted, "I feel like I've really hit a wall. That's why I decided to come to this place. I thought the peace and quiet may help, but... it hasn't worked so far, though."

"Well, you've only been here five minutes," she encouraged. "Give it a chance."

"True," he conceded. "Patience isn't my strong point, though. So, you... you're probably going to put those flowers in water, right?"

"Sorry?" she asked.

"The flowers you picked," he clarified, pointing to them.

"Right, yes," she responded. "Well, I suppose I'll see you around?"

"How about tonight?" he suggested."Do you want to go on a pub crawl?"

"Pubs really aren't my scene, to be honest with you," she admitted. "I'm pretty boring."

"It's not really my scene either, to be honest," he confessed. "I suppose I'm boring, too. Why don't you just come around here? We can be boring together. Perhaps I can cook."

"You cook, do you?" she asked, tilting her head.

"No," he laughed. "But I'm not too bad at ordering a take away or something."

"Yes, that'd be nice," she agreed, a lilt in her voice and a shine in her eyes.

"Great," he exclaimed. "How about eight?"

"Yes, okay," she agreed. "I'll see you then."

"See you then," he replied, a sense of excitement bubbling within him.

As Annie disappeared back to her flat, Ben stood there, contemplating the serendipity of the encounter. The coastal town, with its hidden corners and unexpected companions, already felt more intriguing than he had imagined.

The journey back to his temporary sanctuary took on a different hue. The drizzle that had left the town washed now seemed like a cleansing ritual, washing away the stress of the seagull skirmish. As he entered the manor, he couldn't help but think about the upcoming evening with Annie. A spark of inspiration flickered within him, reigniting the desire to overcome the writer's block that had been holding him captive.

In the quiet solitude, he settled down with his thoughts, the rhythmic sounds of the sea in the distance providing a comforting backdrop. The vibrant images of Brixham, the seagull attack, and the chance encounter with Annie played like scenes from a novel yet to be written. It was a canvas waiting for the strokes of his words to bring it to life.

As the evening shadows began to stretch their fingers across the landscape, Ben found himself eagerly anticipating the simple yet profound pleasure of shared companionship. With the hands of the clock inching closer to eight o'clock, the promise of spending the evening with Annie, accompanied by a comforting takeaway meal and the potential for stimulating conversation, sparked a glimmer of excitement within him. It was a beacon of light, a welcomed respite from the self imposed solitude that had become his familiar companion.

As the vibrant hues of twilight painted the sky above with a soft palette of warm tones, Ben couldn't help but feel that there was more to this coastal town than met the eye. Beyond its picturesque façade, he sensed a depth of untold stories waiting to be discovered, each one offering a glimpse into the rich tapestry of human experiences that unfolded against the backdrop of the sea.

With the daylight bidding its farewell, he embraced the unfolding journey of self-discovery and creative rejuvenation that lay ahead. It was a voyage filled with promise, a canvas upon which he could paint the colours of his dreams and aspirations. With a renewed sense of purpose and a heart brimming with anticipation, he eagerly awaited the serendipitous encounters and unexpected twists of fate that would guide him along this path of exploration and enlightenment.

5

The wax trickled languidly down the carefully positioned candles, resembling the unhurried crawl of snails, while the amber flames swayed gracefully, painting playful shadows that danced across their faces, enveloping the room in a cocoon of tranquillity. As they nestled into the inviting embrace of the plush sofa, a palpable blend of excitement and comfort filled the air, mingling seamlessly with the gentle flicker of candlelight that accentuated every nuance of their expressions.

He wrestled with the words swirling within him, each one vying for attention like waves crashing upon the shore of his consciousness. His thoughts churned tumultuously, a tempest of uncertainty and longing raging within. As he felt his throat tighten and his palms grow damp with nerves, he braved the swirling currents of emotion and ventured forth.

"So, tell me," he began, his voice a tentative beacon in the midst of the storm. "Tell me about yourself, the stories that reside within your heart."

His words, though simple, carried the weight of his desire to unravel the enigma before him, to navigate the uncharted waters of conversation with grace and sincerity.

Her pause was pregnant with introspection, her gaze drifting momentarily into the depths of her own thoughts. A subtle furrow of her brow hinted at the complexity of her inner world, as if she were delicately navigating the labyrinth of her own existence.

With a softness in her voice that mirrored the gentle flicker of a candle flame, she ventured forth. "What facets of my being do you wish to explore?" she inquired, her words a tender invitation to delve deeper into the intricacies of her soul. It was as though she were offering him a map to the secret chambers of her heart, each word a whispered promise of revelation and connection.

"Ah, that's a tough one," he responded, his brows furrowing in thought. "What type of music do you like?"

A playful chuckle danced across her lips, her demeanour suddenly loosening like a flower blooming under the morning sun.

"Well, isn't that just the epitome of corny?" she quipped, her eyes sparkling with amusement.

"Fair point, not exactly setting the stage for greatness," he conceded with a smirk, a hint of laughter bubbling beneath his words. "But hey, let's look at it in another way. How about delving into the treasure trove of childhood memories? Got any favourites to share?"

A mischievous twinkle danced in her eyes as she delivered her playful jab.

"You're starting to sound like a psychiatrist," she teased, a smile playing on her lips. "As for my schooling, let's just say I had the unique privilege of being educated by a group of nuns."

"Ah, the million dollar question," he quipped with a wry grin, his eyebrows arching in playful curiosity. "So, were you the mischievous troublemaker keeping the nuns on their toes?"

A subtle smirk danced across her lips as she tilted her head, a glimmer of mischief sparkling in her eyes. "Believe it or not, I was quite the model student," she asserted with a playful lift of her chin. "No shenanigans from me, I'm afraid. The nuns would vouch for my angelic behaviour, I assure you."

His eyes twinkled with amusement as he leaned back, scratching his jaw thoughtfully. "Almost sounded convincing," he mused, a playful smirk tugging at the corners of his lips. "But let's be real here. Were you just a master of playing the part, or were you genuinely quaking in your boots at the sight of those stern-faced nuns?"

Her words carried a weight of honesty as she spoke, a hint of vulnerability softening her features. "Honestly," she confessed, her voice tinged with a mixture of resignation and lingering apprehension. "Facing the nuns was like a walk in the park compared to the dread of dealing with my parents. They had a knack for instilling fear like no other."

"Quite strict then?" he asked, eyes widening.

"Strict would be an understatement," she replied with a rueful chuckle, her eyes reflecting a mixture of memories and emotions. "Picture this: rulebooks thicker than encyclopaedias, curfews stricter than prison gates, and consequences harsher than the winter chill. That was life under their roof."

She paused, a wistful smile playing on her lips. "But hey, they meant well, I suppose. Tough love and all that. And what about you?"

"What about me?" he asked.

"Were your parents strict?" she inquired.

"No, not at all," he replied. "They nudged me in the right direction, gave me space to find my own way, you know."

"That's really good," she said.

"Yes, they were," he continued. "Together for forty years before they passed on. Did everything together, those two. They even died within a week of each other."

"Does that scare you?" she asked.

"What? Dying?" he asked.

"No," she replied. "The thought of ending up with someone for that long."

"Not really," he said. "I don't think it does. I mean, my parents were together for decades. Went through a lot of challenges and came out on the other side, still in love. I suppose I'd like to find a relationship with that kind of commitment, you know."

"Great," she said.

His confession hung in the air, heavy with the weight of past heartaches and hard learned lessons.

"You see," he began, his voice carrying the weight of vulnerability. "Relationships have been a bit of a roller coaster ride for me. Take my ex-wife, for instance. When we parted ways, we exchanged those familiar words: 'It's no one's fault.' But let's be real here, that's just one of those comforting lies we tell ourselves, isn't it? Someone always carries the burden of blame. In that case, I reckon most of it landed squarely on my shoulders."

He paused, a solemn reflection crossing his features.

"But here's the thing about mistakes—they're the ultimate teachers. I've learned from mine, every misstep etched into my memory like a cautionary tale. And now, as I stand here, I'm determined not to tread the same rocky path again. Call it growth, call it wisdom—I just call it survival."

"Yes, I know exactly what you mean," she replied, exhaling deeply. "So, what do you look for in a woman?"

"That's a good question," he replied. "I don't know. Maybe someone who I can be talking to in a packed restaurant or bar, look up and realize that we've been talking for hours. The place is all cleared out, and we didn't even realize, because when we're together it feels like we're the only two people in the world. Doesn't that make you want to throw up?"

"No, not at all," she replied. "I always say it's not about material possessions or who looks good on your arm at a party." She put her hand on his chest. "It's about what's in here."

"Yes, that's true. So very true," he said, his fingers gently stroking her hair. "So, would you like to stay tonight?" he asked, his eyes penetrating hers.

"Not tonight," she replied, her words tinged with a hint of hesitation.

"That's a shame," he said, his eyes reflecting a mix of disappointment and understanding. "Do you have to be somewhere?"

"No," she replied. "I just don't want to spoil the night by rushing into anything."

"I understand," he said, a gentle smile playing on his lips as he looked at her.

As their eyes locked, time seemed to suspend around them, an unspoken understanding passing between their gazes like a silent symphony. In that fleeting eternity, a magnetic pull drew them closer, their hearts beating in synchrony, echoing the rhythm of their shared desire.

Without a word, they leaned in, their breaths mingling in the space between them, charged with anticipation and longing. Their lips met in a tender union, a gentle exploration of uncharted territories, igniting sparks that danced across their skin like wildfire.

In that soft, lingering kiss, they found solace, comfort, and a whisper of promises yet unspoken. It was more than just a meeting of lips; it was a fusion of souls, an acknowledgement of the undeniable connection that bound them together, transcending time and space.

As they pulled away, their eyes fluttered open, twin reflections of new found intimacy and the unspoken vow of what lay ahead. In that shared moment, they knew that their journey had only just begun, with countless chapters waiting to be written in the unwavering embrace of their love.

"I'll see you soon," he whispered, his voice a tender caress that lingered in the air like a promise waiting to be fulfilled. With those words, he planted a seed of anticipation in her heart, igniting a flicker of excitement that danced in the depths of her soul.

In the soft glow of their shared moment, she felt the warmth of his breath against her skin, a gentle reminder of the closeness they shared. It was a whisper laden with longing, carrying with it the echo of countless possibilities and the assurance of their imminent reunion.

As he spoke, his words wrapped around her like a comforting embrace, weaving a tapestry of anticipation and hope. In that fleeting instant, time seemed to stand still, their connection transcending the boundaries of the physical world.

With a soft smile and a nod, "Good night. See you soon," she said, her heart brimming with anticipation for the moment when they would be reunited once more.

As she stepped out into the crisp night air, the moonlight painted a silvery path before her, guiding her on this journey of possibility. The echoes of their shared laughter lingered in the air, a sweet melody that accompanied her on the solitary stroll, leaving the door open for the next chapter in their unfolding story.

The wax had long melted down the candles, leaving the room in a soft glow of residual warmth.

A sudden realization struck him — he had work to do.

Shaking off the enchantment of the evening, he walked back into the room and settled into a cosy chair, opening his laptop. The soft click of the keys echoed in the quiet room as he immersed himself in the tasks at hand, the flickering candlelight casting a delicate dance on the screen.

The hours passed, and fatigue crept in, weighing down his eyelids. The ambient glow of the laptop provided the only illumination as he drifted into a realm between wakefulness and dreams. The room became a canvas for the dance of shadows, and the only sounds were the gentle hum of the laptop and the distant symphony of the night.

As the night deepened, exhaustion finally claimed him. His head lolled to the side, and the laptop, now forgotten, continued to hum softly. The room transformed into a dream-scape, shadows playing upon the walls like elusive phantoms.

In the midst of this dreamlike state, shadows appeared over him — a doctor and a nurse. The doctor, clad in a white coat, held pliers in hand and advanced towards him with a solemn purpose. The dream unfolded with a sense of inevitability as the doctor leaned in, pliers poised to extract a tooth.

He woke up startled, the echoes of the dream lingering. The room was once again bathed in the gentle glow of the candles, and the remnants of the dream clung to him like a faint mist. Shaking off the surreal imagery, he became aware of a peculiar sensation in his mouth.

With a tentative touch, he explored his teeth, half expecting to find a void where the tooth had been extracted in the dream. But reality prevailed; all teeth were intact. A sigh of relief escaped him as he acknowledged the transient nature of dreams, a fleeting realm where shadows played tricks on the mind.

A distant melody reached his ears, a gentle intrusion into the silent aftermath of the night. The music, a melody he knew beckoned him, pulling him from the clutches of drowsiness. With a yawn, he shut the laptop, the screen dimming and casting the room into darkness once more.

Following the ethereal strains of "*This is the Story of a Starry Night,*" he found himself drawn to a room where an old record player rested. The room itself seemed to breathe with the memories of times long past, and he couldn't resist the magnetic pull of nostalgia. He approached the vintage device, the music growing louder, now a melodic invitation.

With a delicate touch, he lifted the stylus arm and gently placed it back in its cradle, the music ceasing its enchanting dance. He turned off the record player, the silence settling like a soft veil. As he carefully stowed away the vinyl record, he felt a sense of reverence for the echoes of the past held within those grooves.

The room returned to stillness, the only sound the quiet hum of the night outside. The enchantment of the evening lingered in the air, a delicate whisper of shared laughter and stolen kisses. Closing the door to the room, he took one last look at the record player, a silent guardian of cherished memories.

Outside, the moon hung in the velvety sky, a silent witness to the ebb and flow of stories yet to unfold.

The air retained the fragrance of the shared laughter and the subtle promise of their connection. As he stood and stretched, a soft rustle caught his attention.

Turning towards the door, he found a note, delicately placed on the coffee table. The moonlight spilled through the open door, revealing the elegant handwriting that penned the words:

"Thank you for tonight. The laughter, the stories, and the shared moments warmed this room. I look forward to the next chapter of our story. Until then, let the echoes of our laughter linger, and the moonlight guide us on this journey of possibility.

Yours, Annie."

A gentle smile curved his lips as he traced the words on the note, each syllable imbued with the tender essence of their shared moments. In the quiet embrace of the night, he felt the weight of their connection, a delicate thread weaving through the fabric of their lives.

As he lingered over the heartfelt sentiment, he couldn't help but marvel at the beauty of their journey. The night had been a canvas painted with the hues of longing and possibility, each moment a brush stroke in their evolving story.

With the note cradled in his hands, he felt the gentle pull of fate, beckoning him towards the unknown. It was a door left ajar, inviting him to step into the next chapter of their shared adventure.

As he gazed out into the starlit sky, he felt a sense of peace wash over him, knowing that their story was far from over. With a quiet resolve, he tucked the note away, carrying its warmth with him as he ventured into the waiting embrace of tomorrow.

6

Annie hesitated at the doorway, the morning light streaming in, casting a gentle glow in the hallway. The sunlit living room beckoned, and Ben, bathed in the soft morning light, stood as a welcoming silhouette, extending a warm invitation.

"Hi. Come in, do you want a cup of coffee?" His words hung in the air like a comforting melody, an invitation to step into the warmth of his world.

"I don't know, I just... I feel really embarrassed," she admitted, her gaze fixated on an imaginary spot on the floor, as if seeking solace in the patterns of daylight.

"Why?" Ben's voice was a gentle prompt, urging her to open up, to unravel the knots of emotions that bound her.

"What happened between us," she confessed, the weight of unspoken emotions palpable in the room. The morning held a sense of clarity, and her words floated in the sunlit air, creating a canvas for honesty.

She nodded, understanding dawning in her eyes. "I don't normally kiss a guy I've just met like that. I don't know what you must think of me. You must think I'm a slut or something."

Ben interjected quickly, dispelling her fears, "I don't think that at all. I thought we had a great night last night, just talking. It's a rare thing these days."

"I hope you really mean that. I don't want you to think I'm some tart. I felt we had a connection, and I went with it. But I also don't want you to think I'm some frigid little virgin either. Now I think I've given you the wrong impression both ways," she confessed, vulnerability etched across her face like an open book, illuminated by the morning light.

Ben chuckled, breaking the tension that had woven itself into the room.

"What's so funny?" she asked, her eyes searching for understanding in the daylight.

"You," he replied. "It's just... There's just no lying in you, is there? You just lay your troubles out there in the sweetest, most truthful way. That's what I liked about you last night. Well, that's what I like about you right now, in fact."

"My insane vulnerability doesn't make you want to run a mile then?" she questioned, her eyes searching for reassurance in the brightness of the day.

"No. Do you know I've started writing again?" He shifted the conversation, eager to share a new-found joy that had blossomed within him in the morning light.

"That's great," she responded with genuine enthusiasm, the sunlight dancing in her eyes.

"Yeah. I don't think it's a coincidence either," he continued, his words weaving a narrative of hope and inspiration that resonated with the morning's clarity.

"What do you mean?" she asked, her curiosity piqued, the daylight illuminating her inquisitive expression.

"You've awoken something in me, Annie. Something that I thought I had lost a long, long time ago. So, what? Do you want to come in?" he extended an invitation, the atmosphere filled with anticipation, the air charged with the promise of new beginnings in the morning light.

"I can't right now," she admitted, regret shading her features like a fleeting shadow cast by the morning sun.

"But what are you doing today?" he asked, his voice carrying a note of hopeful anticipation. "I'll be here. You can come around any time."

"Yes, okay," she agreed, a hint of a smile tugging at her lips, a flicker of excitement dancing in her eyes in the daylight.

"So, I'll see you later," he said, the promise of shared moments lingering in the morning air, the potential of a new chapter waiting to be written.

"Okay, fine," she said, the acceptance of the invitation lingering in the space between them, bathed in the morning light.

"Hey, Annie," he called out as she turned to leave, his voice carrying a warmth that echoed in the bright hallway.

"Yeah?" she said, turning to face him once more.

"Last night, do you know I was... I was worried it was just a one-time thing, you know," he said, laying bare his vulnerability, his fears exposed in the morning light.

"Not for me, it wasn't," she said, her voice carrying a certainty that dispelled the lingering doubts, like the morning sun burning away the mist.

"Me neither. I'll see you later," he concluded, his smile lingering as she stepped into the day, leaving the promise of a new beginning suspended in the autumn daylight.

The echoes of their conversation intertwined with the rustle of leaves, as if nature itself acknowledged the birth of something extraordinary. The day embraced them, holding the potential for a shared journey that awaited with each step into the sunlight.

As Annie ventured into the day, she found herself wandering through St. Mary's churchyard. The morning sun filtered through the leaves, dappling the path ahead with a mosaic of light and shadow. The air was infused with the fragrance of autumn, and the distant laughter of children playing added to the symphony of the day.

As she strolled along, Annie couldn't shake the warmth of Ben's words and the genuine connection they shared the night before. The morning seemed to carry with it a promise of renewal, of possibilities yet to unfold. She felt a renewed sense of purpose, as if the daylight had illuminated not just the world around her but also the path she wanted to take.

The day unfolded like a tapestry, each moment woven with a sense of adventure and discovery.

In the late afternoon, with the sun beginning its descent, Annie decided to make her way back to the manor. The streets, now bathed in the golden hues of the setting sun, exuded a quiet serenity. She found herself looking forward to the continuation of their conversation, eager to see where the day would lead them.

Upon reaching the manor, she hesitated for a moment before knocking on the door. The echoes of their earlier dialogue still resonated within her, creating a backdrop for the unfolding chapters of their connection. The door swung open, and Ben greeted her with a warm smile, the remnants of daylight playing in his eyes.

"Hey, Annie. Come on in," he said, the anticipation of shared moments palpable in the air. The daylight, now mellowed, cast a soft radiance on their faces as they stepped into the warmth of the manor, ready to explore the possibilities of the evening ahead.

"Do you know, I think Dr. Kendal has come out of his room?" Ben said, a hint of uncertainty in his voice.

Annie, sitting across from him in the dimly lit living room, looked intrigued.

"What makes you think that?"

"The record player's on every night. Also, there's lots of stuff being moved around the house, you know," he replied.

"Creeping you out, is it?" she asked.

"Yeah. A little bit," he replied.

Annie contemplated for a moment. "Maybe you should call the caretaker."

"Yeah, I've been having some pretty vivid dreams as well," he said.

Annie leaned forward, curious. "Like what?"

"Well, there was... there was one where I was drowning. And another freaky number where I'm having my teeth pulled out," he replied. "Well, it sounds crazy, right?"

"If you say it happened, then I believe you," she replied.

"You do?" he asked, raising his eyebrows.

"There's a lot of things in this world we don't understand. I try to keep an open mind about everything," she replied. "So, what are you going to do?"

"Well, I'd like to speak to the lady who looks after the place, that's for certain. Maybe she can shed some light on all of this?" he answered.

Annie nodded, but doubt lingered. "But come on, is she really going to admit there's something strange going on? Even if she did know, I don't think she wants that sort of thing getting out. No one will ever set foot in the place again."

"True. Well, I'd like to speak to Doctor Bloody Mystery, that's for sure," he said.

"You know, if you think there's something paranormal going on, you could get a priest in to bless the place," she said.

"There's the Catholic in you talking," he said.

"Lapsed Catholic," she smiled.

"Yeah. Well, I'm more interested in finding answers, Annie, not bloody purging the place," he said.

"How about a Ouija board?" she asked.

"A Ouija board? That would definitely be a last resort," came his reply.

"Do you want me to stay here with you tonight?" she asked.

"As good as that sounds... No, I'm probably better off just utilizing these creative juices while they're still flowing, you know. I don't know. Perhaps I'm just... losing my mind here or something," he replied.

"You're not crazy," she said. "Sounds like typical anxiety dreams. What are you anxious about? Is it just the man in the annex or..."

"Well, I suppose that's... strange enough, isn't it?" he replied. "But now... Yeah, I was pretty anxious anyway. That's why I came here. London was getting me right down. Too many people, too much hustle and bustle, you know."

Annie listened, understanding. "How come you chose this area?"

Ben's eyes brightened with nostalgia. "I was invited to spend some time here," he replied. "I used to live down the road in Kingswear and I'd come over to Brixham all the time when I was a kid. It's one of the great memories I have with my parents, actually. I can remember they used to pick me up every Friday after school, and we'd just come over, it was great. Part of me wonders why I decided to return I don't know. Am I letting my imagination run away with me here? Plus, I'm just getting the lines between fact and fiction a bit blurred, you know?"

"You don't need to question yourself, Ben. Always trust your instinct. Trust your heart," she said.

"It's lovely here and you're a calming influence on me, Annie, you know that?" he said.

"I try," she said.

" You know, I went to London for the work originally. But truth be told, Annie, I'm really not looking forward to going back there," he continued.

"At least you had your shot at the Big Smoke. I always thought about moving to Bristol or London, but I never did," she said.

"What stopped you?" he asked.

"I'm your typical small town girl," she replied. "I dreamed of the bright lights and the big city, but... I could never make it happen. I'm not bitter though. Sometimes I think the way you're meant to be, you're meant to be."

"Well, you can be whatever you want to be, Annie," he said. " You don't have to go anywhere to achieve it. You can make things happen right here. You don't necessarily have to work for anybody either. You can just do it yourself. You just... Yeah, you gotta believe, yeah."

"You know, I make some of my own jewellery. I thought... I guess I hoped that I could turn that into a business one day," she said.

"Well, you should do that," he said.

"It's not as easy as that though, is it? I've got a creative mind, but not much of a business one," she said, shrugging her shoulders.

"Then perhaps I could help you," he said. " Well, I've written lots of books. Maybe I could help you get into the business mindset of things, yeah?"

"Why would you want to do that?" she asked.

"Because, Miss Tolcher... you have inspired me. And I'd love to return the favour. It'd be great," he replied.

"So the writing's going well then?" she asked.

"Yes. Yes, yes, it really is," he replied, his eyes lighting up. "I came here to write another book that means something to me, you know. Something personal. And I'm... I'm getting there. I'm getting there. I suppose... it's like the more I let go, the freer my mind becomes, you know. Then think of it this way. It might be creepy living with a strange man in the annex, but... it'll make great material for horror readers."

"True," she said.

The room fell into a contemplative silence as they sat surrounded by the dim glow of the table lamp. The soft hum of the record player provided a subtle background melody to their thoughts.

After a moment of contemplative silence, Annie leaned forward, her eyes sparkling with a tantalizing glimmer of excitement, as if she held the key to a treasure trove of hidden secrets. "You know what, Ben?" she began, her voice infused with a new-found sense of adventure. "Perhaps it's time we delve into these enigmas hand in hand. Let's dance with uncertainty, let it become the very pulse of your script."

Ben's gaze met hers, a flicker of intrigue igniting within him like a match catching fire in the dark. Her words seemed to breathe life into his creative spirit, weaving a tapestry of possibilities before his mind's eye.

With a silent nod, he felt the weight of hesitation lift from his shoulders, replaced by a surge of inspiration that begged to be unleashed upon the blank pages of his manuscript.

7

Ben sat hunched over his laptop, his concentration broken only by the rhythmic tapping of keys. The soft glow of the screen cast a warm light in the dim room. As he delved into his work, a fleeting shadow danced across the periphery of his vision.

His heart raced within the confines of his chest, its rhythm akin to a relentless drumbeat echoing through the cavernous silence of the dimly lit room. The once serene landscape depicted in the painting which hung above the fireplace now lay askew on the floor, its colours mingling in a chaotic dance that seemed to taunt his bewildered gaze.

He stood motionless, ensnared in a web of disbelief and apprehension, his thoughts darting through a maze of possibilities in search of a rational explanation for the inexplicable event. Could it be a mere play of light, or perhaps a sudden gust of wind from an open window? Yet, as he stared at the fallen artwork, a cold shiver ran down his spine, for deep within him, a gut wrenching certainty whispered that no mundane explanation could justify the eerie movement.

Each step toward the painting felt like a hesitant plunge into the unknown, the air thick with anticipation as though the very walls of the manor held their breath in anticipation.

With trembling hands, he reached down to retrieve the fallen masterpiece, his fingers hesitantly tracing the familiar contours of the canvas as if seeking solace amidst the chaos.

"Did you see that?" His voice pierced the stillness, reverberating through the room with a chilling intensity, though he knew he stood utterly alone. The words hung in the air, filled with uncertainty, echoing off the walls like spectral whispers in the night.

The silence that ensued was not merely absence of sound; it was a palpable entity, thick and suffocating. It descended upon him like a shroud, enveloping his senses in a suffocating embrace that seemed to stifle even the beating of his own heart. Each passing moment felt like an eternity, marked only by the shallow intake of breath as he strained to discern any response from the empty darkness.

Yet, the void remained unyielding, its oppressive weight bearing down upon him with relentless force. It was as if the very air had turned to lead, pressing against him from all sides, rendering movement impossible and thought fleeting.

In that moment, he felt a primal urge to flee, to escape the suffocating grip of the silence that threatened to consume him whole. But rooted to the spot, he remained, haunted by the lingering echo of his own words, and the chilling realization that he was not as alone as he had once believed.

Setting the painting aside, he moved forward with deliberate steps, his senses heightened by a mixture of anticipation and trepidation. Each footfall echoed softly against the polished floorboards, a stark contrast to the thunderous drumming of his heart within his chest.

Approaching the fireplace, his gaze swept across the walls like a detective scouring a crime scene for elusive clues. Every inch was scrutinized with meticulous care, as if seeking out the faintest whisper of evidence in a vast expanse of silence. Yet, the walls yielded nothing but their stoic indifference, betraying no hint of the secrets they may conceal.

With cautious fingertips, he traced the edges of the fireplace mantle, half-expecting to encounter a hidden lever or concealed compartment. But the smooth surface offered no resistance, its pristine façade offering no solace to his restless mind.

His eyes lingered upon the fallen painting, the tranquil scene now a distorted reflection of the unease gnawing at his insides. What had once been a peaceful landscape now seemed to exude a sinister aura, its colours muted and its forms twisted into grotesque caricatures of their former selves.

"Okay, this is getting ridiculous," he muttered under his breath, though the feeble protest held no sway over the mounting sense of dread that gripped him. With each passing moment, the weight of the inexplicable events that had unfolded bore down upon him like a suffocating blanket, smothering reason and inviting madness.

He could no longer deny the palpable strangeness that permeated every corner of his once-familiar abode. From inexplicable drafts that whispered secrets in the dead of night to shadows that seemed to move of their own accord, the signs of intrusion were impossible to ignore.

With a heavy sigh, he resigned himself to the reality he had long avoided. The time for denial had passed; now, he must confront the enigma that had invaded his life with relentless persistence. For buried within the heart of this mystery lay answers that he dared not imagine, waiting to be unearthed by a mind brave enough to seek them out.

He awkwardly returned the painting to its place.

Out of the blue, a sharp rap echoed through the quiet of the manor, shattering the stillness like a stone cast into a placid pond. The sound jolted him from his reverie, setting his pulse racing with a mixture of curiosity and apprehension.

With a determined stride, he crossed the room, each step a deliberate echo of his resolve. As he reached the threshold and swung open the door, a rush of cool air greeted him, carrying with it the tantalizing scent of rain and possibility.

Standing there, he found himself face to face with the unknown, a silent sentinel guarding the boundary between his world and whatever lay beyond. Yet, in that moment, there was no room for hesitation or doubt; only the unyielding call of destiny, beckoning him forward into the unknown.

With steady hands, he grasped the handle and pulled the door open, revealing a scene bathed in the soft glow of twilight. And as he stepped into the doorway, he knew that whatever awaited him on the other side, he would face it with unwavering courage and an indomitable spirit.

"Hey, Annie," he greeted as the familiar face greeted him from the other side, relief washing over him like a wave crashing against the shore. The mere sight of her brought a semblance of comfort in the midst of uncertainty. "I know this might sound crazy, but I need your help."

Annie's brow furrowed in concern, her gaze probing his with a mixture of apprehension and curiosity. With hesitant steps, she crossed the threshold into the dimly lit living room, her presence casting a faint glow against the shadows that lingered like silent spectators.

"You sound pretty freaked out," she observed, her voice laced with empathy as she took in the atmosphere of tension that hung in the air like a heavy fog. Her eyes darted around the room, as if seeking solace in the familiarity of their surroundings or searching for elusive answers hidden within the depths of the shadows.

Ben guided Annie to the fireplace, their footsteps echoing softly against the hardwood floor as they approached the scene of the inexplicable event. The painting hung askew on the wall, its once serene landscape now a disconcerting reminder of the unsettling occurrences that had disrupted the tranquillity of the manor.

"I was just sitting here, working on my laptop," Ben began, his voice tinged with a hint of trepidation. "When I saw it move."

His words hung in the air, heavy with the weight of the truth he struggled to comprehend.

"It lifted off the hook and slid down the wall, like it was being moved by something."

Annie's brow furrowed in confusion as she scrutinized the painting, her expression a reflection of the bewilderment that churned within her.

"That's... bizarre," she murmured, her voice barely above a whisper, as if afraid to disturb the fragile veil of normalcy that separated them from the unknown.

"Have you noticed anything else strange happening lately?"

Ben nodded, a shiver coursing down his spine as he recalled the unsettling events that had plagued his once peaceful abode.

"Yeah, there have been other things too," he admitted, his words punctuated by the heavy silence that enveloped them. "Like doors slamming shut on their own, and... weird noises in the middle of the night."

In that moment, the weight of their shared unease hung heavy in the air, binding them together in a silent pact to confront the enigma that had invaded their lives. And as they stood there, illuminated by the flickering glow of the fireplace, they knew that whatever lay ahead, they would face it together, drawing strength from the unbreakable bond of friendship in the face of the unknown.

Her brows furrowed in a look of concern, a shadow crossing her features as her eyes narrowed with apprehension.

"Okay, this definitely sounds like more than just a coincidence," she remarked, her voice barely above a whisper, as if afraid to disturb the ominous stillness that hung heavy in the air.

"We need to figure out what's going on here."

Their determination firm, they embarked on a thorough investigation, scouring every nook and cranny of the room in search of elusive answers. Each step was deliberate, each movement guided by the shared conviction that the truth lay hidden somewhere within the confines of the manor's walls. Yet, despite their best efforts, they found no trace of the paranormal forces that seemed to lurk just beyond their reach.

"I don't understand," Ben muttered, frustration seeping into his voice as he cast a bewildered glance around the room. "How is any of this possible?"

Annie's gaze softened with empathy as she reached out to place a comforting hand on his shoulder, her touch a reassuring anchor amidst the tumult of uncertainty.

"Sometimes, the answers aren't easy to come by," she offered, her voice a soothing balm to his frayed nerves. "But we'll figure this out together, I promise.

In that moment, their bond strengthened by the shared resolve to unravel the mysteries that besieged them, they stood as a united front against the unknown, drawing strength from each other as they braved the uncertain depths of the paranormal realm. And though the path ahead was fraught with peril and uncertainty, they faced it with unwavering courage, secure in the knowledge that together, they were stronger than any darkness that dared to threaten their resolve.

But even as she spoke, an eerie chill seemed to descend upon the room, suffusing the air with a palpable sense of foreboding. Ben's muscles tensed involuntarily as a shiver rippled down his spine, a primal instinct warning him of impending danger. His gaze snapped towards the fireplace, heart pounding in his chest, only to witness the painting tremble ominously on the wall.

"Annie, look!" he exclaimed, his voice tinged with urgency as he pointed towards the artwork. "It's happening again!"

Sure enough, the painting lifted off the hook once more, this time with a violent jerk that sent shock waves of terror rippling through the room. They stood frozen in horrified fascination, their breath caught in their throats as they watched the spectral display unfold before their eyes, the painting seeming to float through the air as if propelled by an unseen force.

And then, as suddenly as it had begun, the movement ceased, leaving behind a heavy silence that hung in the air like a shroud. With a soft thud, it dropped to the floor, the sound reverberating through the room like a funeral toll.

Annie's eyes widened in realization, her features drawn taut with dread. Her voice, barely a whisper, cut through the silence like a knife.

"There's something in this place," she murmured, her words heavy with the weight of their implications. "And whatever it is... it's not happy."

In that moment, the gravity of their situation loomed large, casting a dark shadow over their once peaceful existence. With uncertainty gripping their hearts like a vice, they knew that they were no longer mere inhabitants of the manor, but unwitting participants in a chilling game of survival against forces beyond their comprehension. And as the echoes of their words faded into the oppressive silence, they braced themselves for the harrowing trials that awaited them in the depths of the night.

Ben's heart raced in his chest, the frantic rhythm echoing the turmoil that churned within him as he stood transfixed by the fallen painting. A cold dread gripped his insides, a heavy weight settling in the pit of his stomach like a stone sinking into murky depths. Whatever malevolent force haunted the place, it was abundantly clear that he was grappling with something far more sinister than he had ever dared to imagine.

The eerie silence that hung in the air seemed to thicken around him, suffocating in its oppressive embrace. Each passing moment felt like an eternity, the shadows lengthening in the dimly lit room like tendrils of darkness reaching out to ensnare him in their grasp. And as he stood there, enveloped in the unsettling stillness, he couldn't shake the gnawing sensation that he was merely scratching the surface of the true horrors that lurked within these walls.

Every creak of the floorboards, every whisper of the wind outside, seemed to taunt him with the knowledge of his own vulnerability. With each heartbeat, he felt the looming presence of an unseen malevolence, a sinister force that lurked just beyond the edge of his perception, waiting to strike when least expected.

In that moment, he realized that he was no longer a mere bystander in the unfolding nightmare; he was a participant, entangled in a web of darkness from which there seemed to be no escape. And as the shadows deepened and the night stretched on, he braced himself for the horrors that awaited him in the darkness, knowing that the true battle had only just begun.

"I think it's better that you go home," he said to Annie. "It isn't safe for you here."

"I can't leave you alone," she said, shaking.

"I'll be okay," he said. "Now please go."

As night descended once more, the world outside plunged into a realm of shadows and whispers, a haunting symphony of darkness that seemed to seep into every crevice of his consciousness. He lay in bed, surrounded by a suffocating stillness that echoed the emptiness of his own thoughts. Sleep eluded him, like a distant memory slipping through his fingers, leaving him to wrestle with the demons that prowled in the depths of his mind.

Tossing and turning beneath the weight of his own apprehension, he found himself ensnared in a restless dance with insomnia. Each moment stretched out interminably, the silence broken only by the erratic rhythm of his heartbeat, a relentless drumbeat that echoed the cacophony of his racing thoughts.

Visions of darkness and despair danced behind his closed eyelids, painting vivid tapestries of terror that played out against the canvas of his imagination. Shadows writhed and twisted in the corners of his mind, their tendrils reaching out to ensnare him in a web of fear and uncertainty.

The weight of the unknown pressed down upon him like a leaden blanket, suffocating his every thought and drowning him in a sea of doubt. With each passing moment, the boundaries between reality and nightmare blurred, until he found himself adrift in a realm of half formed dreams and waking nightmares.

In the stillness of the night, Ben grappled with the spectres of his own fears, wrestling with the darkness that threatened to consume him whole. And as the hours slipped away into the abyss, he knew that sleep would remain elusive, leaving him to navigate the labyrinth of his own mind alone, haunted by the echoes of his own uncertainty.

As the hours stretched on and sleep continued to elude him, he felt the weight of responsibility settle upon his shoulders like a heavy mantle. He couldn't afford to succumb to fear; he had to confront whatever lurked in the shadows, to uncover the truth behind the strange occurrences that plagued him.

With a resolve as unyielding as steel, he rose from his bed and navigated the familiar path back to the living room. The darkness seemed to retreat before him, yielding to the unwavering determination that fuelled his every step.

Standing at the centre of the room, he remained poised, his senses keenly attuned to the stillness of the night.

Then, as if in response to his silent challenge, he heard it—a mere whisper, a ghostly echo that slithered through the darkness like a serpent's hiss. "Ben..." The voice, barely audible above the hushed breath of the night, sent a chill coursing down his spine, a primal instinct warning him of impending danger.

Summoning his courage, he called out into the void, his voice trembling with uncertainty. "Who's there?" But his words echoed unanswered, swallowed by the vast expanse of emptiness that surrounded him.

Alone in the darkness, he felt the presence of something sinister, a malevolent force that lingered just beyond the reach of his senses. With every nerve on edge, he scanned the shadows for any sign of movement, any hint of the unseen menace that threatened to consume him.

Yet, despite his vigilance, there was nothing—only the oppressive silence of the night, punctuated by the faint rustle of curtains in the breeze. He realized then that he faced an adversary unlike any other, an enemy that defied conventional means of combat.

With a sinking feeling in the pit of his stomach, he understood that he couldn't rely on brute strength or weapons to vanquish this darkness. No, he would need something far greater—courage, determination, and an unwavering resolve to confront the unknown.

In that moment, his fear gave way to a fierce determination to uncover the truth and banish the darkness that threatened to engulf him. For he knew that he was not alone; he had the strength and the will to face whatever horrors awaited him in the shadows, armed with nothing but his indomitable spirit and an unyielding faith in his own resilience.

8

After the enigmatic encounter with the painting, he decided a hot shower might help clear his mind. The bathroom, with its vintage fixtures, offered a brief escape from the inexplicable events unfolding in the manor.

As the warm water cascaded over him, Ben felt the tension in his shoulders melt away. The rhythmic hum of the shower became a soothing backdrop, momentarily drowning out the perplexing whispers of the manor.

Lost in thought, he turned the tap to release a stream of steam. As the mist curled around the bathroom mirror, he closed his eyes and relished the serenity of the moment. However, when he opened them again, his reflection was distorted by an unsettling message.

"MURDER."

The word, etched in the condensation, sent a chill down Ben's spine. He shook off the unease, attributing it to the stress of the day. Yet, as he continued his shower, a nagging feeling lingered in the air.

Stepping out of the shower and grabbing a towel, he paused to glance at the mirror. The mist had transformed into an ominous proclamation. His eyes widened as he noticed drops of crimson staining the pristine white surface of the hand basin.

His heart raced, the manor's whispers now growing louder. An inexplicable fear seized him as he wrapped the towel around his waist. The door, previously bolted shut, now hung ajar, creaking ominously in the still air.

Startled, Ben approached the door cautiously, his breath catching in his throat. Before he could react, the door slammed shut with a resounding bang, echoing through the silent manor. Panic set in as he tugged at the doorknob, desperate to escape the confining space.

"Is someone there?" he called out, his voice wavering. No response echoed back, only the eerie silence of the manor.

Turning away from the stubborn door, Ben noticed the bolt had mysteriously retracted. The once-sealed entrance now swung open, leaving him bewildered and unnerved. He hesitated, unsure of what to make of the bizarre sequence of events.

Little did he know that the manor's secrets were far from revealed. A faint whisper lingered in the air, carrying an otherworldly message that would propel Ben deeper into the mysteries that surrounded the old estate.

As the mysterious events unfolded, Ben couldn't shake the feeling that the manor had become a character in its own story—a story woven with threads of the past, secrets, and a subtle invitation to unravel the enigma within its walls.

The air inside held a tangible anticipation, as if the manor itself was leading him down a winding path of discovery. The soft rustle of curtains and the distant murmur of unseen voices added to the eerie atmosphere, creating an ambiance that bordered on the supernatural.

The discarded painting was just the beginning. Each room, every nook and cranny, whispered tales of bygone eras, lost loves, and untold tragedies. Ben found himself drawn deeper into the historical tapestry of the manor, unable to resist the allure of its haunting allure.

Late at night, as the manor settled into an eerie silence, he would hear faint echoes of laughter and the melancholic strains of a piano. Ghostly apparitions danced in the corners of his vision, leaving him questioning the thin veil between the living and the spectral.

With each passing day, the manor seemed to reveal more of its secrets. Hidden passages, concealed doors, and forgotten chambers emerged, as if the house itself was guiding Ben through a labyrinth of time. The very architecture became a living testament to the stories it harboured.

As Ben delved into old documents and faded photographs, he unearthed a tale of love and betrayal, of a family torn apart by circumstances beyond their control. The manor had been a silent witness to generations of joy and sorrow, and Ben became an unwitting archivist, piecing together the fragments of a narrative etched in the very walls.

As the moon cast an eerie glow over the sprawling grounds of Upton Manor, Ben found himself drawn deeper into its mysteries. Each creak of the old floorboards seemed to whisper secrets of the past, and as he traced his fingers over the antique furnishings, he couldn't shake the feeling of being watched by unseen eyes.

But it was the inexplicable message etched in the condensation on the mirror that truly sent shivers down his spine – the stark word "MURDER" looming ominously before him. It hung in the air like a chilling omen, leaving Ben grappling with questions that clawed at the edges of his consciousness.

Was this a mere trick of the elements, or was the manor itself trying to communicate with him? Could it be that within these walls, a sinister deed had been committed? The very thought sent a shudder through him, igniting a relentless curiosity that refused to be quelled.

Who had met their untimely end within these hallowed halls? And more importantly, who had wielded the hand of fate? The whispers of the past seemed to echo louder now, urging Ben to uncover the truth buried beneath layers of deception and time.

With each passing moment, the weight of the mystery pressed upon him, driving him to delve deeper into the shadows that clung to Upton Manor like a cloak of darkness. The answers lay waiting, obscured by the veil of history, and Ben knew that he alone held the key to unlocking the secrets that had long been concealed within these hallowed walls.

As he delved deeper into the manor's history, he discovered a hidden room, untouched by time. In its centre stood an ornate, antique desk covered in dust. Among the yellowed pages of a forgotten journal, he found the confession of a long-forgotten soul—a confession that painted a macabre tableau of jealousy, revenge, and a life cut short.

The discovery sent shivers down his spine, and the manor seemed to sigh with relief, as if the truth had been set free. The revelations didn't end there; instead, they opened a gateway to the unknown, beckoning Ben to explore the realms of the supernatural that permeated the very fabric of the place.

With each revelation, the bond between Ben and the manor deepened. He became not just an occupant but a custodian of its stories, a bridge between the living and the departed. The manor, once a mere dwelling, had transformed into a portal to the past, inviting those willing to listen to the echoes of history that resonated within its time-worn walls.

As the days passed, the mysteries entrenched within the walls of Upton Manor gradually unveiled themselves, like ancient scrolls unfurling their secrets to the curious eyes of those who dared to decipher them. Ben found himself drawn deeper into the enigma, his curiosity piqued with every revelation, every whispered rumour that echoed through the corridors of the old estate.

It began with subtle hints—an inexplicable draft that chilled the air, whispers of long-forgotten voices lingering in the shadows, and the occasional glimpse of movement in the corner of his eye, only to vanish when he turned to look. Yet, these were mere breadcrumbs leading him into the labyrinthine depths of Upton Manor's secrets.

As he delved deeper, Ben unearthed tales of generations past, each one adding a layer to the intricate tapestry of the manor's history. Stories of forbidden romances, tragic betrayals, and whispered pacts made under the moon's watchful gaze painted a picture of a past shrouded in secrecy and intrigue.

But it was not just the stories of yore that captured Ben's imagination; it was the tangible remnants of the past that still lingered within the manor's walls. Hidden passages concealed behind tapestries, cryptic symbols etched into the stone, and locked doors guarding untold treasures—all hinted at a past that refused to stay buried.

Driven by an insatiable thirst for knowledge, Ben embarked on a quest to unravel the mysteries of Upton Manor, each revelation bringing him closer to the truth yet simultaneously deepening the veil of uncertainty that shrouded the estate.

And so, beneath the watchful gaze of the moon and the silent guardianship of the ancient oaks that surrounded the manor, Ben journeyed further into the heart of darkness, determined to uncover the secrets that lay hidden within Upton Manor's hallowed halls. For he knew that only by unlocking the secrets of the past could he hope to find the answers he sought—and perhaps, in doing so, finally bring peace to the restless spirits that wandered its corridors.

9

The room exuded an unsettling calmness, as if time itself had paused to observe the scene unfolding within its confines. The only disruption to this eerie tranquillity was the subtle protest of the aged floorboards, protesting Ben's careful steps as he placed the Ouija board upon the table.

With a mixture of trepidation and amusement, he took a moment to survey his surroundings, his breath catching in his throat. The flickering candlelight cast dancing shadows upon the walls, enhancing the ominous atmosphere of the room. Yet, amidst the palpable tension, a nervous chuckle escaped his lips, a testament to the surreal absurdity of the situation he found himself in.

As he prepared to delve into the mysterious realms of the occult, a sense of anticipation tingled in the air, mingling with the lingering echoes of his laughter. Little did he know, the events about to unfold would shatter the delicate balance between scepticism and belief, plunging him into a world where the boundaries between reality and the supernatural blurred into obscurity.

"Hello, Mr. Ouija board," he muttered, almost mockingly. The air hung heavy with doubt as he prepared to embark on a journey into the unknown.

"All right," he sighed, his tone laced with frustration. "Fuck it."

Despite the cynicism clouding his mind, he pressed on, his fingers lightly resting on the planchette.

"Spirit guides, guardian angels of light...I call upon you to answer my question."

A wave of self-consciousness washed over him, and he couldn't help but mutter under his breath, "This is so fucking stupid."

Yet, as if in response to his plea, an inexplicable force seemed to guide his hands. The planchette moved, spelling out the cryptic message, "It works."

A shiver raced down his spine, sending a cascade of goosebumps rippling across his skin, as his gaze remained fixed upon the ominous board before him. With each passing moment, the weight of the supernatural reality looming over him grew heavier, threatening to engulf him in its enigmatic embrace.

As if guided by an unseen hand, the room underwent a startling transformation, bathed in an ethereal glow that seemed to emanate from the very heart of the Ouija board itself. Shadows twisted and contorted upon the walls, their movements erratic and unsettling, as if they were dancing to an unearthly melody.

Ben found himself entranced by the surreal spectacle unfolding around him, his senses heightened to the point of exhilaration and fear. Every creak of the floorboards, every flicker of the candle flame, seemed to carry a deeper, more profound meaning, as if the very fabric of reality were unravelling before his eyes.

In that moment, he realized that he stood at the precipice of something far greater than himself, something ancient and powerful, waiting to be unleashed upon the world. And as he braced himself to confront the unknown, he couldn't help but wonder what secrets lay buried beneath the surface of the seemingly innocent Ouija board.

"The painting above the fireplace...is there any significance to it?" he inquired, his voice barely a whisper.

"Death," the board spelled out, sending a chill down his spine.

Ben's mind raced with questions. "Did someone die here?"

The planchette moved to "No," then slowly and deliberately spelled out "Sharkham Point."

Dread settled over the room as he pressed on, the anticipation gnawing at him.

"The record player. Who keeps on turning on the record player?" he asked. "Did anybody use to listen to the player? Anybody who lived here?"

Nothing.

"Please...Who used to listen to the record player?" he asked again.

"Adrian," the board answered, sending a shock wave through Ben's being.

"Who is Adrian?" he questioned further.

"Adrian," it answered.

Ben's frustration grew. "Who is Adrian? Come on, please. Tell me, who is Adrian?"

"Dr Kendal," came the answer.

The planchette moved with an uncanny assurance.

"Murderer. Adrian. Sharkham Point."

A chill swept through the room, and Ben's heart pounded. "Is Dr Kendal a murderer? Who did he murder?"

The planchette hesitated before spelling out, "Stop it."

Desperation crept into Ben's voice. "Stop it! Stop it, all right! Stop it! Stop it!"

The room seemed to pulse with energy, and Ben's plea echoed in the emptiness. "Stop it. I've had enough of this shit! Please."

The planchette lay still, the atmosphere returning to an uneasy calm. Ben's mind raced with the revelation, his scepticism battling against the inexplicable events. Little did he know that the journey into the mysteries of the supernatural had only just begun, leaving him teetering on the edge of a realm where the veil between the living and the dead was thin and fragile.

As he sat there, beads of sweat formed on his forehead, he couldn't shake the feeling that he had opened a door to something beyond his comprehension. The room, now eerily silent, held a lingering tension as if the very air pulsed with unseen forces. And on the other side of the locked door leading to the annex, the mysterious Dr. Kendal.

A moment of uncertainty hung heavy in the air, as Ben stood on the threshold of a decision that would shape the course of his fate. Should he press forward, delving deeper into the mysteries that beckoned from beyond the veil of the ordinary? Or would he retreat, seeking refuge in the comforting embrace of the familiar, banishing the enigma before him to the recesses of his mind?

His gaze lingered upon the Ouija board, its surface now appearing deceptively benign, yet pulsating with an unseen energy that seemed to tug at the very fabric of his being. It lay before him like a dormant gateway, offering a passage to realms beyond comprehension, each letter and symbol etched upon its surface a tantalizing invitation to unravel the secrets of the unknown.

In the turmoil of his thoughts, Ben found himself torn between opposing forces, his heart pulled in conflicting directions by the allure of the supernatural and the comfort of the mundane. The desire for answers warred with the instinct for self-preservation, each vying for dominance within the confines of his soul.

With a furrowed brow and a clenched jaw, he grappled with the weight of his decision, acutely aware of the consequences that lay in wait on either path. For to embrace the mysteries that lay before him was to risk losing himself in their depths, to surrender to the intoxicating allure of the forbidden. And yet, to turn away would be to forsake the chance to uncover truths that eluded him, condemning him to a life of perpetual ignorance and uncertainty.

In the end, as the echoes of his inner turmoil reverberated within the chamber of his mind, he knew that there could be no turning back. With a resolute determination that belied his trembling hands, he reached out, his fingers hovering over the surface of the Ouija board, ready to embark upon a journey into the unknown. For in that moment, he understood that true enlightenment could only be found by confronting the darkness that lurked within the shadows.

The silence was broken by a distant, disembodied whisper that seemed to murmur through the walls, leaving him on edge.

"Stop it," it echoed, a haunting reminder of the mysteries that lingered in the shadows.

He took a deep breath, his eyes fixed on the Ouija board. "What now?" he whispered to himself, unsure if he was ready for the answers that lay beyond.

The room held its secrets, and the thin veil separating the living from the dead left him teetering on the precipice of the unknown.

As he pondered his next move, the record player crackled to life, its haunting melody filling the room. His eyes widened, his heart racing, as if the spirits themselves were orchestrating a symphony of enigma.

The air grew charged with an ethereal energy, leaving his imagination to question whether his journey into the supernatural had just begun or if he had unwittingly unleashed forces beyond his control. The possibilities loomed like shadows in the dark corners of the room, inviting speculation and anticipation.

Little did he know that the spirits he had invoked might have plans of their own, and the consequences of meddling with the occult could spiral into a series of events that would challenge the boundaries of the living and the dead.

The Ouija board, now a conduit between two worlds, held the key to unravelling a tale that transcended time and mortality.

As he stared into the unknown, the unanswered questions hung in the air, leaving him to wonder what twists and turns awaited him in the chapters yet to unfold. The supernatural realm beckoned, and the story of his encounter with the mysterious forces was poised on the brink of an unpredictable and chilling odyssey.

The room, once a sanctuary of scepticism, now pulsated with a palpable energy, each corner harbouring the secrets of the afterlife. Ben, caught between curiosity and fear, felt the weight of the unseen world pressing on him. The Ouija board, an innocent game turned channel to the supernatural, seemed to beckon him further into the enigma.

Hours passed, the room cloaked in a mystic ambiance as he delved deeper into his quest for understanding. The planchette glided across the board, revealing fragments of a tale that transcended the boundaries of the living and the dead. The whispers of spirits echoed in the air, leaving him to decipher the cryptic messages that unfolded before him.

As the night wore on, the atmosphere grew thick with anticipation. Shadows danced on the walls, seemingly choreographed by the unseen forces at play.

The air, charged with an otherworldly energy, carried with it the weight of untold stories.

Driven by an insatiable curiosity, Ben continued his dialogue with the spirits. Each question unravelled a new layer of the mysterious narrative. The room became a theatre of the supernatural, with Ben as both the audience and the unwitting protagonist.

"The painting above the fireplace," he inquired once more, his voice steady despite the mounting tension. "What does it signify?"

The planchette responded with deliberate movements, spelling out a tale of passion, betrayal, and an untimely demise.

He listened intently, his mind racing to piece together the fragments of the spectral puzzle.

"Adrian," he ventured cautiously, returning to the enigmatic figure that had surfaced earlier. "Who is Adrian, and why does his name echo through these spectral whispers?"

The planchette glided smoothly, weaving a narrative that transcended the boundaries of the corporeal realm. Adrian, it seemed, was a key player in a tragic tale of love and loss, forever etched into the fabric of Upton Manor.

Dr. Kendal's name resurfaced in the ghostly conversation, his association with Adrian now taking on a sinister hue. The revelation of murder hung in the air, casting a chilling shadow over the room. Ben, now entrenched in a supernatural saga, grappled with the weight of the revelations.

The record player, dormant for a while, sprang to life with an otherworldly melody. Its haunting notes intertwined with the ethereal whispers, creating a symphony that resonated with the stories of the past. The room, now a stage for the supernatural, held its breath as if caught in a temporal vortex.

Ben's mind, a whirlwind of emotions and revelations, faced a critical juncture. The Ouija board, a tunnel to the unknown, held the key to unlocking the mysteries of Upton Manor. The question lingered, echoing in the stillness of the room: Would he delve deeper into the enigma or retreat from the uncanny realm he had uncovered?

With each passing moment, the boundary between the living and the dead blurred further. The whispers grew louder, the shadows more pronounced, and the room itself seemed to breathe with an unearthly pulse.

As he grappled with his decision, the spirits seemed to anticipate his next move. The planchette, now an instrument of spectral guidance, moved with purpose, spelling out a cryptic message: "The threshold awaits, Ben. Cross it, and the mysteries shall reveal themselves."

The air became charged with a potent energy, a harbinger of the supernatural climax that awaited. The room, now a nexus of spectral forces, held its breath as Ben stood at the crossroads of the known and the inexplicable.

In the ensuing silence, the echoes of Upton Manor's tragic history reverberated. The room, a sanctuary turned supernatural theatre, awaited the protagonist's decision—the threshold of revelation beckoning, and the chapters of the unknown ready to unfold.

The Ouija board, now an instrument of spectral revelation, seemed to pulse with an otherworldly energy. The planchette, guided by unseen hands, hovered over the board, awaiting his decision.

As the whispers of the manor's tragic tale lingered in the air, Ben faced a pivotal choice. The threshold, a metaphysical doorway, beckoned him to unravel the mysteries that clung to the fabric of the old building. The room, caught in a spectral embrace, held its breath, mirroring the anticipation that hung in the balance.

"Cross it," a disembodied whisper seemed to echo, reverberating through the room. The decision weighed heavy on his shoulders, his every heartbeat resonating with the rhythm of an uncharted journey.

With a hesitant breath, he extended his fingers toward the planchette, the cool surface sending a shiver down his spine.

The Ouija board responded with a surge of energy, its letters forming a cryptic message: "Seek the truth, Ben."

The room, now charged with a delicate ambiance, seemed to expand beyond its physical confines. Shadows played on the walls, dancing to the rhythm of an unseen force. The record player, an unwitting conductor, emitted haunting melodies that intertwined with the whispers of the supernatural.

As Ben ventured into the unknown, the air thickened with anticipation. The planchette glided across the board, spelling out fragments of the spectral narrative. Adrian, Dr. Kendal, and Sharkham Point became intertwined in a tapestry of tragedy, each revelation pulling Ben deeper into the enigma.

"Adrian had a secret love," the planchette spelled out, unravelling a tale of forbidden passion and a love that defied the boundaries of life and death. The room, now a theatre of the supernatural, cast its spell on Ben, drawing him further into the spectral web.

Questions flooded his mind. How did Adrian's secret love lead to murder? What secrets did Upton Manor harbour beneath its quaint façade? The Ouija board, now a link to the past, held the key to unlocking the truth.

The room seemed to blur at the edges, its boundaries fading into the unknown. Ben felt a spectral presence, an unseen audience witnessing the unravelling of a tale that transcended time. The threshold, once a metaphorical divide, now became a tangible reality, and he hesitated on the brink of revelation.

A sudden gust of wind swept through the room, extinguishing the candles that had flickered with an eerie glow. Darkness enveloped him, and the room echoed with a deadly silence. The Ouija board, now an indistinct silhouette in the obscurity, awaited the next chapter of the supernatural saga.

As he stood in the darkness, the only source of illumination came from the faint glow of the moon casting its silvery light through the window. Shadows morphed into ethereal shapes, and the room became a canvas for the spirits to paint their spectral tale.

The record player, now silent, echoed with a ghostly resonance. The haunting melody lingered in the air, a melancholic soundtrack to the unfolding mystery. The whispers of the manor's tragic history murmured through the void, leaving an indelible mark on the room and its reluctant protagonist.

With a tentative step, Ben moved toward the window, drawn to the moonlit night outside. Upton Manor, nestled in the embrace of darkness, held secrets that transcended the boundaries of the living and the dead. The Ouija board, a relic of the supernatural, remained at the centre of the room, its letters obscured by the shadows.

As he gazed into the night, a single word echoed in his mind: "Adrian." The enigmatic figure, entwined in a tale of passion and tragedy, beckoned him to uncover the truth. The journey into the mysteries of Upton Manor had just begun, and Ben found himself entangled in a spectral dance that defied the logic of the mortal realm.

The room, once a haven of scepticism, had transformed into a magnet for the supernatural. Shadows whispered the secrets of the past, and the air crackled with an energy that transcended the mundane. The moon, a silent witness to the unfolding drama, bathed the manor in a mystical glow.

As Ben surrendered himself to the enigmatic embrace of the night, he felt the palpable weight of uncertainty settle around him like a cloak of shadows. Every step forward seemed to echo with the irreversibility of his decision, each movement a testament to the courage required to delve deeper into the abyss of the unknown. With a silent determination, he turned his attention to the Ouija board, its mystic surface a canvas of possibilities, now rendered mute yet pregnant with anticipation.

Within the confines of the room, darkness reigned supreme, its velvety shroud enveloping everything in its embrace. It was as if the very air held its breath, straining against the veil of obscurity, awaiting the imminent unveiling of secrets that lay dormant within the walls of Upton Manor. The spectral inhabitants, mere echoes of lives once lived, hovered on the threshold of existence, their ethereal presence adding an eerie ambiance to the already charged atmosphere.

As Ben's fingers hovered over the planchette, he could sense the energy in the room shifting, a subtle yet undeniable ripple in the fabric of reality. Each moment held the promise of revelation, each motion of the planchette a potential gateway to truths both profound and chilling. With a mixture of trepidation and curiosity, he embarked on a journey that would not only shape the destiny of Upton Manor but also unravel the mysteries of its spectral denizens, forever altering the course of his own fate.

10

Ben's footsteps echoed softly against the aged floorboards of the dimly lit room within the sprawling manor. His mind was a tempest of thoughts, each one grappling with the unsettling occurrences that had besieged him within these walls. The haunting melodies emanating from the vintage record player only added to the oppressive atmosphere, casting eerie shadows across the room. Yet, it was the cryptic writing etched onto the fogged surface of the bathroom mirror that truly sent shivers down his spine.

As he paced, his mind raced, seeking rational explanations for the inexplicable events that had unfolded. But try as he might, he found himself ensnared in a web of uncertainty and unease. It was as if the very air around him was thick with secrets, whispering of things unseen and unexplained.

Unable to shake off the palpable sense of dread that clung to the house like a shroud, he knew he had to seek answers. And in a moment of clarity, his gaze settled upon an unexpected source — Mrs. Parkes, the stoic caretaker who oversaw the day-to-day operations of the estate.

Though hesitant, he resolved to confront Mrs. Parkes, hoping she might shed light on the mysteries that plagued the manor.

With a hesitant breath, he grasped the phone tightly in his trembling hand, his fingers hovering over the familiar digits that would connect him to Mrs. Parkes. The faint hum of the manor's surroundings seemed to intensify, casting an eerie backdrop to his already fraught nerves. Each dial tone echoed through the room like a harbinger of uncertainty, amplifying the weight of his decision.

Finally, the connection buzzed to life, and Ben held his breath as he awaited a response. His pulse quickened with each passing second, each heartbeat drumming in his ears like a warning. And then, like a beacon cutting through the darkness, Mrs. Parkes' voice echoed through the phone, her tone as enigmatic as ever, yet somehow comforting in its familiarity.

"Hello?" she intoned, her voice a soothing balm against the backdrop of unease that had enveloped him. And in that moment, as their words hung suspended in the air between them, Ben knew that he had taken the first step towards unravelling the mysteries of the manor. But little did he know, the answers he sought would only plunge him deeper into the labyrinth of secrets that lay hidden within its walls.

"Hello, Mrs. Parkes. It's Ben Sanders here at the manor."

"Oh, hello. How's it going there?" she asked.

"Yeah, look, I just wanted to ask you a couple of questions. They might seem a little strange." he said.

"I'm intrigued."she said.

He approached the subject with caution, his words measured and deliberate, unsure of how she would receive his revelations. The air between them crackled with tension, thick with the weight of the unspoken, as he cautiously described the peculiar happenings that had unsettled him to his core.

"Well, it's just about this place. I was wondering if you ever had any previous residents mention unusual occurrences?"

"Like what?" she asked.

"Occurrences of the supernatural," he replied.

The moment stretched taut, the weight of anticipation heavy in the air, as he awaited her response. It seemed as though time itself held its breath, suspended in the stillness of the room. Then, like the breaking of a dam, her reply shattered the silence, flooding the space with her measured words.

"No. Are you looking for material for a book, Mr. Sanders?" she asked.

"No. It's nothing like that. It's just that there's been some unusual things happening in the house that I'm really struggling to find a rational explanation for." he replied.

Mrs. Parkes, her demeanour poised and unyielding, delved deeper, her inquisitive nature leaving no stone unturned as she pressed for precise details.

"Can you be more specific?" she asked.

"Well... Well, the record player often comes on in the night by itself. And there's stuff being moved around the house. And I was in the shower earlier on and... Writing appeared on the mirror just before the door slammed and locked me in." he replied.

"Well, that's quite a story. You writers have wonderful imaginations." she said.

"Oh, no, no, no. It's just that I'm trying to find out what's happening. I thought perhaps, I don't know, it could be linked to the history of the place. Have you ever heard of any incidents happening down the years or anything?" he asked.

Mrs. Parkes, maintaining a composed demeanour, assured him, "Of course I haven't. Nothing that I know of."

Ben, desperate for any lead, turned his attention to the mysterious figure in the annex.

"So... I hope that this man in the annex, Dr. Kendal, is there anything at all you can tell me about him?" he asked.

"I'm sorry, but I can't divulge personal information. I'm sure you can appreciate that. I don't think you'd like it if I blabbed your..." came her reply.

"Yes, of course. I'm sorry to bother you," he said.

The call concluded with a sombre echo, leaving Ben engulfed in a maelstrom of frustration. Despite his relentless pursuit, the elusive information remained just beyond his grasp, as the manor steadfastly guarded its enigmatic secrets, shrouded in an impenetrable veil of mystery.

As he mulled over the conversation, a sense of isolation settled in. The manor, with its creaking floorboards and flickering lights, seemed to watch him with silent anticipation. The mysteries that cloaked the building only deepened, leaving him at the crossroads of the known and the unknown.

With a sigh, he contemplated his next move. The manor, like a silent witness to its own enigma, held the key to a narrative that unfolded in whispers and shadows. The night stretched before him, with the promise of revelations and the weight of the unknown.

Despite the unsettling nature of the call, he couldn't shake the feeling that he had merely scratched the surface. The manor, with its history veiled in secrecy, beckoned him to delve deeper into its spectral embrace. The journey into the unknown had just begun, and the chapter that unfolded held the promise of unravelling the mysteries that clung to the very fabric of the old place.

The night pressed on, and Ben found himself drawn deeper into the enigmatic web that surrounded the manor. The air inside the old edifice seemed to thicken with every passing minute, and the echoes of Mrs. Parkes' words lingered in the dimly lit room.

Restless, he decided to explore the manor further, guided by an insatiable curiosity and an unyielding need for answers. He ascended the creaking staircase, the wooden steps groaning beneath his weight, and entered a corridor adorned with faded wallpaper that whispered tales of bygone eras.

Each door along the corridor beckoned with the possibility of uncovering secrets. He hesitated, his hand hovering over the tarnished doorknobs, contemplating the mysteries that lay beyond. The manor seemed to pulse with a quiet energy, as if it held its breath, waiting for someone to unveil its hidden narratives.

As he opened the doors one by one, the rooms revealed themselves like chapters in a forgotten storybook. Dust danced in the air, catching the faint moonlight that filtered through moth eaten curtains. His footsteps echoed through the silent chambers, each one a reverberation in the timeless symphony of the manor.

In one room, he discovered an antique writing desk adorned with yellowed papers and quill pens. The musty scent of aged parchment filled the air, and he couldn't resist leafing through the faded pages. The room, frozen in a bygone era, seemed to whisper tales of forgotten aspirations and untold dreams.

In another room, he stumbled upon a collection of sepia toned photographs. Faces from the past stared back at him, frozen in moments of joy, sorrow, and everything in between. The eyes in the photographs seemed to follow him, as if imploring him to unravel the threads that connected their lives to the manor.

As he continued his exploration, he entered a room at the end of the corridor that exuded an ominous aura. The door creaked open with a reluctance that sent shivers down his spine. Inside, he found a dimly lit space adorned with dusty furniture covered in white sheets.

A portrait on the wall caught his attention — a stern-faced man with penetrating eyes. The plaque beneath read "Dr. Adrian Kendal." The discovery sent a chill down Ben's spine, realizing that this was the same Dr. Kendal he had inquired about with Mrs. Parkes. The mysterious Dr. Kendal locked away in the annex.

The room seemed to hum with an otherworldly resonance, as if the very walls held memories of a tumultuous past. Ben's gaze lingered on the portrait, and he couldn't escape the feeling that the eyes of Dr. Kendal bore witness to the secrets concealed within the manor.

In the midst of his exploration, a faint sound reached his ears — the distant strains of a piano. Intrigued, he followed the melody that seemed to drift through the corridors, guiding him to a forgotten room on the upper floor.

The door creaked open to reveal a room bathed in a soft, ethereal light. A grand piano stood in the centre, its keys untouched by human hands for years. Yet, the haunting melody persisted, as if played by unseen fingers.

The room resonated with the echoes of a bygone era, and Ben found himself captivated by the spectral symphony. The manor, it seemed, was alive with the whispers of its past residents, and the piano became a vessel for the unspoken stories that lingered in the air.

As he stood in the ghostly glow of the piano room, he realized that the manor held more than mere physical dimensions. It was a repository of memories, a tapestry woven with threads of joy, sorrow, love, and tragedy. The boundaries between the living and the dead blurred, and the manor became a threshold to a realm where time was an ever flowing river.

The night wore on, and Ben, enveloped in the mysteries of the manor, felt a profound connection to the spirits that dwelled within its walls. The journey into the unknown had become a pilgrimage through time, and each room he explored revealed a new chapter in the spectral narrative.

As he descended the staircase, the piano's melancholic melody still lingering in the air, he knew that the manor held secrets that transcended the limits of his understanding. The answers he sought were elusive, yet the journey had become an odyssey into the heart of its enigma.

The manor, with its creaking floorboards, faded wallpaper, and silent echoes, beckoned Ben to continue his exploration. The night, heavy with the weight of untold stories, unfolded like a tapestry of the supernatural. And so, the chapter continued, with each step revealing the layers of the manor's haunting history.

As Ben delved deeper into the manor's mysteries, he discovered a hidden door concealed behind a dusty tapestry.

The door, reluctant to yield, opened to reveal a narrow staircase leading to a dimly lit cellar. Intrigued by the prospect of unravelling more secrets, He descended into the subterranean realm.

The cellar exuded a palpable sense of antiquity, the air heavy with the scent of aged wood and dampness. The flickering light of his mobile phone revealed ancient wine barrels, forgotten relics, and a myriad of forgotten artefacts. Amongst the relics, a peculiar chest caught his eye.

As he cautiously opened it, a collection of weathered journals emerged. The journals, filled with handwritten entries, chronicled the lives of past residents and the tumultuous history of Upton Manor. Ben, engrossed in the pages of the journals, discovered tales of love, betrayal, and a series of unexplained deaths that had plagued the manor.

One entry, dated decades ago, spoke of Dr. Adrian Kendal, a prominent figure. The journal hinted at a forbidden romance between Dr. Kendal and a mysterious figure. The illicit affair had stirred gossip among the town's residents, and tragedy had befallen Upton Manor in its wake.

The more he delved into the journals, the more he realized that the manor was a silent witness to the intertwining fates of its inhabitants. The spirits of the past seemed to echo through the cellar, their voices reaching out to him as he pieced together the puzzle of the manor's haunting history.

As he reached the final pages of the journals, a sudden gust of wind swept through the cellar and the light on his mobile phone went out. In the ensuing darkness, the whispers of the past grew louder, as if the spirits themselves were guiding him through the concluding chapters of the enigmatic tale.

With trepidation, he ascended from the cellar, the weight of the revelations settling on his shoulders. The manor, once a mere backdrop to his mundane existence, had transformed into a nexus of the supernatural, a conduit between the living and the dead.

Emerging into the moonlit night, Ben realized that the answers he sought were entwined with the very fabric of its history. The manor, now a sanctuary of spectral memories, beckoned him to continue the exploration into the unknown.

The night sky, adorned with a tapestry of stars, watched over it as he stood at the crossroads of revelation. The journey into the manor's mysteries had become an odyssey, and the chapters yet to unfold promised a resolution to the spectral enigma that had haunted the place for generations.

As he walked through the shadowy corridors, the whispers of the past faded into the ethereal melody of the piano, still resonating through the halls. The spirits, it seemed, were not confined by the limitations of time, and their stories lingered in the air like echoes of a bygone symphony.

The manor, with its hidden passages, forgotten journals, and spectral whispers, had become a living testament to its interwoven destinies. Ben, now a reluctant protagonist in the unfolding saga, embraced the uncertainty of the journey ahead.

And so unfolded the chapter of his journey, each footstep echoing through the corridors of the supernatural realm. The manor, its secrets unfurling like tendrils of mist in the moonlight, beckoned him deeper into its embrace. It stood as an ancient sentinel, its walls resonating with the weight of history, offering glimpses into the enigmatic tapestry of the past to those bold enough to heed its call and listen to the faint whispers carried on the breeze of time.

11

As the sun dipped low on the horizon, its warm rays cascaded over tranquil Higher Brixham, casting a mesmerizing palette of gold and amber upon the landscape. The streets, worn smooth by centuries of footsteps, wound their way through its heart, bordered by quaint, old buildings adorned with ivy and blooming flowers, creating an ambiance of timeless elegance.

Amidst this picturesque scene, the churchyard of St. Mary's lay nestled in a quiet corner, its ancient gravestones standing as silent sentinels amidst the sea of greenery. Here, history whispered through the rustling leaves, weaving tales of bygone eras and the lives of those who had once walked these hallowed grounds. Shadows danced among the tombstones as the breeze carried the secrets and stories of generations past, lending an aura of mystique to the sacred space.

In the fading light of the evening, its charm seemed to deepen, each corner holding within it a fragment of the town's rich tapestry of history and lore. And as the sun dipped below the horizon, painting the sky with hues of crimson and violet, the beauty of Higher Brixham, with its timeless streets and storied churchyard, remained etched in the hearts of all who beheld it.

Ben, a spirited young man with an insatiable thirst for exploration and a soul ablaze with the fire of adventure, found himself inexplicably pulled towards the serene allure of the cemetery. It stood as a sanctuary of paradoxes, a realm where the realms of existence and oblivion converged in an endless waltz, where the echoes of bygone lives reverberated through the stillness of the air.

Stepping into the sacred enclave of St. Mary's, an aura of reverence enveloped him, sweeping over his senses like a gentle tide. The atmosphere was imbued with a solemn serenity, the air tinged with the subtle fragrance of wild flowers mingled with the earthy essence of the soil. As he ventured deeper into the heart of the cemetery, a symphony of contrasts unfolded before him.

The sunlight filtered through the canopy of ancient trees, casting intricate patterns of light and shadow upon the moss covered tombstones that stood guard over the hallowed grounds. Each weathered marker bore witness to the passage of time, their surfaces etched with the stories of lives once lived, now immortalized in stone.

Amidst the tranquil beauty of St. Mary's, the boundary between the realms of the living and the departed seemed to blur, creating an ethereal landscape where the spirits of the past danced alongside those who still drew breath. It was a place where the veil between worlds grew thin, where whispers of the beyond echoed through the rustling leaves and the shifting shadows.

In the midst of this haunting beauty, he felt a profound sense of connection to something greater than himself, as if the very essence of the cemetery reached out to touch his soul.

Here, amidst the quietude of St. Mary's, he found himself immersed in a timeless realm where the mysteries of life and death intertwined in a delicate dance, inviting him to ponder the fleeting nature of existence and the enduring legacy of the human spirit.

He wandered aimlessly through the graveyard, his senses alive to the sights and sounds that surrounded him. Every corner held a story, every gravestone a silent testament to lives once lived. But it was in the older section of the cemetery that he found himself inexplicably drawn to a particular weathered and worn tombstone bearing the name Annie Tolcher. The name sent a shiver down his spine, awakening memories that lay dormant in the recesses of his mind. Where had he heard that name before? What secrets did it hold? For a moment, he couldn't shake the feeling of déjà vu, as if he had stumbled upon a fragment of a dream long forgotten.

With trembling hands, he traced the letters of Annie Tolcher's name, as if seeking solace in the cold embrace of stone. The inscription on the tombstone was faded but still legible, a poignant reminder of the life that once was - *Annie Tolcher, Rest in Peace.*

But beneath the surface of those seemingly innocuous words lay a mystery waiting to be unravelled. Who was she, this Annie Tolcher, whose name lingered like a whisper on the lips of time? What circumstances had consigned her to this quiet corner of the world, her story obscured by the passage of years? As the day waned and the shadows deepened, Ben found himself consumed by a relentless curiosity, his mind awash with questions and conjectures.

Lost in a labyrinth of thoughts, he conjured visions of Annie's life – a young woman adorned with aspirations and dreams, her laughter a melody that once danced through the cobblestone streets of the town. Yet, amidst the tapestry of his imaginings, darker threads began to weave themselves into the fabric of her narrative. What tragedies had befallen her, what secrets had she harboured beneath her façade of serenity?

Driven by an insatiable hunger for truth, Ben resolved to plunge headlong into the enigma of Annie Tolcher's existence. With each step through the sombre aisles of the cemetery, he felt the weight of history pressing down upon him, urging him onward in his quest for understanding.

As he retraced his path toward the churchyard's entrance, Ben cast a lingering glance over his shoulder at the weathered tombstone, its secrets still veiled in shadow. The mystery it held remained a tantalizing enigma, a puzzle waiting to be pieced together in the recesses of the old churchyard.

With a silent vow etched upon his heart, he stepped out into the embrace of the cool night air, the stars above guiding his way like celestial beacons. But just as he prepared to depart, a voice shattered the silence, freezing him in his tracks and setting his pulse alight with anticipation. "Are you visiting Annie, too?"

Ben turned to see a figure emerging from the shadows – a young woman with eyes as dark as wet earth, her face framed by waves of shining hair. It was Annie Tolcher.

Taken aback, Ben could hardly believe his eyes. The lady he had gotten to know over the past few days, the one who had captured his heart with her laughter and kindness, shared the same name as the mysterious person whose tombstone he now stood before.

"You... you're Annie Tolcher?" he stammered, his heart pounding in his chest.

The young woman nodded, a sad smile playing at the corners of her lips. "Yes, that's me. Well, my name, at least."

Ben's mind reeled with confusion. How could this be possible? What strange twist of fate had brought them together in this haunting place?

As if sensing his turmoil, Annie stepped forward, her gaze searching his face with a mixture of curiosity and concern. "Is everything okay? You look like you've seen a ghost."

Ben shook his head, trying to make sense of the whirlwind of emotions swirling inside him. "It's just... I didn't expect to meet you here. I mean, with the same name and all..."

Annie's smile softened, and she reached out to touch his arm gently. "I know, it's a bit strange, isn't it? But I feel a connection to this place, to the memories it holds. It's like... like I'm drawn to it somehow."

Her words struck a chord within Ben, resonating with the inexplicable pull he had felt towards the cemetery ever since he had arrived in St. Mary's. Could it be that they were both drawn here by the same unseen force, by the echoes of the past calling out to them across the years?

With a new found sense of purpose, Ben looked into Annie's eyes, his determination renewed. "Let's uncover the truth together," he said, his voice steady with resolve. "Let's unravel the mystery of Annie Tolcher and discover the secrets hidden within these ancient grounds."

She nodded, her eyes shining with determination. "Together," she echoed, her voice filled with a quiet strength that stirred something deep within his soul.

Under the twinkling canopy of the night sky, where constellations whispered secrets of ages long gone, Ben and Annie's footsteps echoed through the ancient corridors of the churchyard. Moonlight filtered through the dense foliage, casting ethereal shadows that danced around them like ghostly spectres. Each step they took seemed to unravel another layer of the enigmatic tapestry that bound their destinies together.

As they ventured deeper into the heart of the graveyard, the air thickened with a palpable sense of anticipation, as if the very earth held its breath in anticipation of what was to come. Above them, the stars shimmered like diamonds strewn across the velvet canvas of the heavens, bearing witness to the unfolding drama below.

Hand in hand, they navigated the maze of weather-worn tombstones, their fingers intertwined as if seeking solace in each other's touch amidst the eerie stillness. Around them, the spirits of the past seemed to stir, their whispers carried on the gentle breeze that rustled through the ancient trees.

But amidst the haunting beauty of the night, there was also a sense of urgency, a feeling that time was slipping away like grains of sand through an hourglass. For Ben and Annie, this journey was not merely a stroll through a graveyard; it was a quest to uncover the mysteries that lay buried beneath centuries of history.

With each passing moment, the bond between them grew stronger, fuelled by a shared determination to unravel the secrets of the past. And as they stood together, beneath the watchful gaze of the stars, they knew that whatever trials lay ahead, they would face them as one, their love a beacon of light in the darkness of the unknown.

12

As Ben traversed the echoing corridors of Upton Manor, an eerie sensation tugged at the corners of his consciousness, hinting at the untold tales veiled within its ancient walls. Each creaking floorboard seemed to murmur secrets of generations past, enticing Ben deeper into the labyrinth of curiosity.

One tranquil afternoon, as the fading sunlight painted elongated shadows across the dimly illuminated passageways, Ben's insatiable curiosity led him to a previously unexplored chamber. The air hung heavy with anticipation, as though the very atmosphere held its breath, awaiting the revelation of hidden truths within the enigmatic confines of the room.

As the door groaned open on rusty hinges, it unveiled a chamber seemingly frozen in the annals of time. Golden specks of dust pirouetted in the slanting rays of sunlight, lending an otherworldly aura to the space. He stepped over the threshold, his senses ensnared by the musty scent of antiquity that permeated the air.

His gaze swept across the room, drawn inexorably to a singular focal point: an imposing painting adorning the weathered walls. Time had not diminished its commanding presence; rather, it imbued the artwork with an aura of aged grandeur. At its centre stood the figure of Dr. Kendal, enigmatic and enshrouded in mystery, his likeness rendered with an artist's meticulous hand.

He approached the painting, his pulse quickening with each step, as though drawn by an invisible thread woven through the fabric of time itself. The eyes of Dr. Kendal seemed to follow his every movement, their depths concealing untold secrets and untamed mysteries. It was as if the very essence of the elusive figure reached out from the canvas, beckoning him into a realm where reality blurred with the realms of legend and lore.

As his gaze lingered upon the intricately detailed portrait, his scrutiny unveiled a startling revelation that sent a shiver coursing down his spine – standing at Dr. Kendal's side was a young woman, her presence etched into the canvas with a haunting familiarity. The resemblance she bore to Annie, with her delicate features and cascading curls, was so uncanny that it seemed as though time itself had folded upon itself.

Blinking in disbelief, he rubbed his eyes, half expecting the apparition to dissipate like a wisp of smoke. Yet, as his vision cleared, the image remained steadfast, each brush stroke immortalizing the enigmatic connection between the woman in the painting and his beloved Annie. It was as though the very essence of Annie had been captured in the pigment and canvas, a spectral echo reaching across the ages to bridge the chasm between past and present.

A tumult of emotions surged within him – disbelief mingled with wonder, curiosity entwined with trepidation. Could this be a mere coincidence, a trick of the light playing upon his senses, or did it hint at deeper, more profound truths buried within the labyrinthine corridors of Upton Manor? With trembling hands, he reached out as if to touch the spectral visage, his heart pounding with a mixture of apprehension and longing, yearning to unravel the mysteries veiled within the enigmatic portrait.

As his gaze traced the contours of the woman's flowing gown, he couldn't shake the feeling that it possessed an ethereal quality, as if woven from threads spun by ancient spirits. Each fold and crease seemed to dance with a life of its own, rippling like the surface of a tranquil lake stirred by a gentle breeze.

But it was her eyes that held him spellbound, twin pools of dark wet earth that mirrored the vivacious curiosity he had often seen gleaming in Annie's gaze. It was as if the very essence of her had been captured in the pigment, her spirit imbuing the portrait with a vibrancy that transcended the confines of canvas and paint. And her smile – oh, that enchanting smile – it radiated warmth and familiarity, drawing him into its embrace with an irresistible magnetism.

A whirlwind of thoughts spun through his mind, each one a fragment of the puzzle he struggled to piece together. How could the woman in the painting, with her uncanny resemblance to Annie, exist centuries before his beloved had ever graced the halls of Upton Manor? Was it mere coincidence, or did it hint at a deeper, more enigmatic connection threading its way through the tapestry of time?

Lost in a labyrinth of uncertainty, Ben found himself torn between rational scepticism and the tantalizing allure of the unknown. Could the woman in the painting hold the key to unlocking the secrets hidden within Upton Manor's hallowed halls? With a furrowed brow and a heart heavy with unspoken questions, he resolved to delve deeper into the enigma that bound him to both past and present, determined to uncover the truth that lay veiled beneath layers of history and mystery.

Annie had been his steadfast anchor amidst the swirling enigma that was Upton Manor. Her laughter, like a cascading stream of sunlight, had echoed through the dim corridors, banishing the oppressive shadows that clung to the ancient estate. In her presence, the looming mysteries of the manor seemed to lose their grip, replaced by a warmth and familiarity that enveloped him like a comforting embrace.

Their budding romance had blossomed like a rare flower amidst the thorns of uncertainty, each stolen moment a precious respite from the enigmatic forces that conspired to keep them apart. With Annie by his side, Ben had felt invincible, as though together they could unravel the secrets hidden within the very walls of Upton Manor.

But now, faced with her spectral likeness immortalized in a centuries-old painting, his sense of reality trembled on the precipice of disbelief. How could the vivacious young woman he had come to know and love exist simultaneously in the present and the distant past? Was it merely a trick of fate, a cruel twist of destiny designed to test the limits of his sanity?

As he stood before the haunting portrait, the weight of uncertainty bore down upon him like a leaden cloak, threatening to stifle him in its suffocating embrace. With trembling hands and a heart heavy with the burden of unanswered questions, Ben struggled to reconcile the tangible reality of Annie's absence with the spectral presence that now loomed before him. In that moment, the line between illusion and truth blurred, leaving him adrift in a sea of swirling uncertainty, grappling with the enigma that had come to define his very existence.

Transfixed by the painting's mesmerizing tableau, Ben's gaze swept over the scene, his mind wrestling with a tumult of conflicting emotions. There, captured in the strokes of the artist's brush, stood Dr. Kendal and Annie, their figures frozen in a moment of timeless intimacy amidst a verdant garden.

A sense of disbelief mingled with fascination as he traced the contours of their forms, the lines of their features etched with an eerie precision that seemed to defy the passage of time. The garden, lush and vibrant, teemed with life, each blossom and blade of grass imbued with a vitality that belied the desolate stillness of the manor's surroundings.

But it was the enigmatic energy that seemed to pulse from the canvas, an invisible current that sent shivers racing down his spine. It was as if the very essence of that fleeting moment had been distilled into pigment and canvas, trapping Dr. Kendal and Annie in a space between past and present.

The clash of vibrant colours against the backdrop of the mansion's sombre façade lent the scene an unsettling harmony, like a discordant melody played in perfect unison. It was a juxtaposition that spoke to the underlying tension that permeated Upton Manor, a dichotomy of beauty and decay that mirrored the enigma of its inhabitants.

As Ben continued to study the painting, a sense of foreboding crept over him, a gnawing uncertainty that whispered of hidden truths waiting to be unearthed. With each passing moment, the boundaries between reality and illusion blurred, until he found himself standing on the precipice of a revelation that promised to reshape his understanding of

Upton Manor and the mysteries that lay within its haunted halls.

His thoughts churned like a tempestuous sea as he stood before the enigmatic portrait, grappling with the unsettling revelations it stirred within him. How, he wondered, was Annie inexorably linked to Dr. Kendal, a figure shrouded in the veils of Upton Manor's murky past? And why, of all the subjects that could have been immortalized in paint, was it Annie who stood beside the elusive doctor, her presence etched into the very fabric of the canvas?

The romantic tendrils that had entwined Ben and Annie's lives, once thought to have bloomed solely in the realm of the present, now seemed to transcend the boundaries of time itself. Their connection, he realized with a dawning sense of awe, reached back through the annals of history, weaving a tapestry of love and mystery that spanned centuries.

As he grappled with these unsettling truths, he felt as though he stood at the crossroads of two divergent realities – one grounded in the tangible present, and the other steeped in the enigmatic depths of Upton Manor's labyrinthine past. The lines between past and present blurred, until they merged into a singular continuum of existence, where the echoes of bygone eras reverberated through the hallowed halls of the ancient estate.

With each passing moment, his understanding of the world he thought he knew shifted, reshaped by the inexorable pull of history and the mysteries that lay buried beneath layers of time and memory. And as he stood amidst the swirling currents of uncertainty, one thing became abundantly clear – the answers he sought lay not only in the present, but in the tangled web of Upton Manor's past, waiting to be unravelled by a seeker bold enough to brave its haunted depths.

With a steely resolve burning in his chest, Ben forged ahead into the depths of the chamber, his footsteps echoing against the time worn floorboards. As his eyes adjusted to the dim light, he found himself surrounded by rows of dusty tomes, their once-vibrant spines now cracked with the weight of centuries.

Each book held the promise of untold revelations, their yellowed pages a testament to the passage of time. With trembling hands, he reached out, pulling volumes from their resting places with a reverence reserved for sacred artefacts. The air was thick with the scent of ancient paper, mingling with the musty aroma of forgotten secrets that lingered in the air.

As he pored over the brittle pages, he unearthed a trove of relics from Upton Manor's past – crumbling letters bound in ribbon, faded photographs capturing moments long since lost to memory. Each artefact whispered of lives intertwined, of loves lost and betrayals concealed beneath the veneer of respectability.

It soon became evident that Upton Manor was more than just a labyrinth of twisting corridors and hidden passageways; it was a repository of history, a custodian of the countless stories that had unfolded within its walls. Beneath the façade of architectural grandeur lay the echoes of lives lived and connections forged in the shadows of its storied past.

With each discovery, Ben felt the tendrils of the enigma tightening around him, drawing him ever deeper into the heart of Upton Manor's mysteries. It was a journey fraught with peril and uncertainty, but he knew that he could not turn back.

For the answers he sought lay buried within the labyrinthine depths of the manor, waiting to be unearthed by a soul bold enough to brave the darkness that lay concealed within its ancient halls.

With each step deeper into the recesses of Upton Manor, Ben felt the weight of history pressing down upon him, its whispers echoing in the corridors of his mind. The portrait of Dr. Kendal and Annie loomed large in his thoughts, its enigmatic presence a silent sentinel guarding the gateway to the past.

As he studied the painting, a realization slowly unfurled within him like the petals of a long-forgotten bloom.

The figures in the portrait stood as silent witnesses to the passage of ages, their gazes locked in a timeless embrace that transcended the boundaries of mortality. Dr. Kendal, with his inscrutable expression, and Annie, with her lively countenance, seemed to beckon Ben into the depths of their intertwined destinies, inviting him to peel back the layers of history that shrouded their connection in mystery.

It was as though the portrait itself held the key to unlocking the secrets of Upton Manor, its silent tableau serving as a bridge between past and present, reality and illusion. With each stroke of the artist's brush, the threads of fate had been woven into the fabric of the canvas, binding Dr. Kendal and Annie together in a dance of destiny that spanned the ages.

As Ben stood before the portrait, he knew that he stood at the threshold of a journey that would test the limits of his courage and resolve. The whispers of the past beckoned him onward, promising revelations that lay hidden beneath the surface of Upton Manor's hallowed halls. And with a determined heart and a steady hand, he stepped forward, ready to embark on a quest that would unravel the mysteries of time and bring the truth to light.

What was once merely a backdrop now seemed to pulse with an otherworldly energy, as if the very walls of the manor were alive with untold stories waiting to be unravelled. Shadows danced across the walls, their movements whispering of hidden truths and ancient mysteries.

With each hesitant step forward, Ben found himself drawn deeper into the heart of the room, like a moth to a flame. The air crackled with anticipation, every breath tinged with the weight of centuries-old secrets waiting to be unearthed. Unbeknownst to him, he had crossed a threshold into a realm where the line between reality and the supernatural blurred into obscurity.

As he ventured further into the labyrinth of shadows, the boundaries between the known and the unknown began to dissolve, leaving him teetering on the precipice of enlightenment and madness. In this crucible of revelation, every corner held the promise of discovery, but also the threat of a truth too profound for mortal comprehension.

Unaware of the forces at play, Ben pressed on, driven by a curiosity that bordered on obsession. Little did he realize that in his quest for understanding, he was risking more than just his sanity. For in the depths of the manor's secrets lay a power that defied mortal understanding, waiting to consume those who dared to seek its truth.

As he stepped into the depths of Upton Manor, he felt the weight of centuries pressing down upon him, each brick and beam whispering its own tale of bygone days. The chapters of the manor's storied history unfolded before him, written not in ink alone, but in the echoes of footsteps long faded, and the whispers of those who once walked these hallowed halls.

The room seemed to breathe with a life of its own, an ancient energy coursing through its veins and beckoning him further into its depths. Shadows danced upon the walls like spectres of the past, weaving a tapestry of secrets that begged to be unravelled. With each step, he felt as though he were being drawn deeper into a labyrinth of mystery, guided by an unseen hand through the annals of time.

The air crackled with a palpable sense of anticipation, as if the very atmosphere itself was charged with the electricity of discovery. His heart quickened in response, echoing the rhythm of suspense that enveloped him like a cloak. It was as though he had stepped into a world suspended between reality and fantasy, where every corner held the promise of revelation, and every shadow concealed a hidden truth.

Unwavering in his determination, he pressed forward, his senses heightened by the intoxicating thrill of the unknown. For in this moment, he was not merely a visitor to Upton Manor, but a seeker of its deepest secrets, poised on the precipice of revelation. And as the ancient walls whispered their secrets to him, he knew that he was about to embark on a journey that would forever alter the course of his destiny.

As he delved deeper into the mysteries of Upton Manor, he couldn't shake the sensation that the very fabric of the estate was woven with threads of love, betrayal, and unfulfilled destinies. Each artefact in the room seemed to harbour its own tale, whispering secrets that mingled with the echoes of the past resonating through the corridors.

As the sun dipped lower, casting elongated shadows that danced upon the walls like restless spirits, Ben's resolve hardened. The enigma of Dr. Kendal and Annie beckoned to him like a siren's call—a story waiting for its storyteller, a puzzle begging to be solved. With each revelation, he felt as though he held the quill to write another chapter in the saga of Upton Manor, drawing himself inexorably deeper into the shadows of eternity.

His exploration transcended mere curiosity; it had become a pilgrimage into the very heart of an intricate tapestry of secrets. The room, now a sanctum of revelations, pulsed with a life force all its own. Dust motes swirled in the slanting sunlight, performing an ethereal ballet that mirrored the elusive secrets cradled within the manor's walls.

Annie, once a beacon of warmth in the shadows of Upton Manor, now stood at the epicentre of a narrative spanning generations. The bond between her and Dr. Kendal defied the constraints of time, blurring the lines between the living and the spectral. The portrait on the wall captured a love that had transcended mortality, its melancholic beauty hauntingly poignant.

With each revelation, the room seemed to tighten its grip on Ben, ensnaring him in the enigma of Upton Manor. Shadows deepened, and the air grew thick with the weight of untold stories, as if the very essence of the estate conspired to reveal its secrets yet remained just beyond reach.

In a forgotten alcove, he unearthed a weathered diary belonging to a long-forgotten soul. The ink had bled into the pages, merging the lines between joy and sorrow. The author spoke of a forbidden love affair, clandestine meetings beneath the moonlit boughs of Upton Manor's gardens. Though names were veiled in cryptic language, the descriptions painted vivid scenes that resonated with a haunting familiarity.

Annie's laughter, once a balm to the eerie silence, echoed through the annals of time. The burgeoning romance between Ben and Annie seemed to echo a tale that had unfolded before, a cyclical dance of passion and tragedy transcending the bounds of mortality.

As the last vestiges of sunlight faded, Ben's determination swelled. The mysteries of Upton Manor were no longer mere shadows but a living, breathing entity, urging him to unravel the threads binding past and present. The room throbbed with an ethereal energy, as if the very walls were imbued with the memories of those who had sought solace within its confines.

With each revelation, the intensity of the chapter heightened. Ben's hands trembled as he turned the pages, uncovering the poignant narratives weaving together the lives of Upton Manor's denizens. The room, once a silent observer, now stood as a confessional, compelling Ben to decipher the cryptic messages left behind by those who had traversed its halls.

As the shadows lengthened and night draped its cloak over the manor, Ben realized he had become an integral part of its story. The untold secrets whispered through the air, and the weight of history bore down upon him. The journey into the shadows of eternity had only just begun, and with every step, Ben moved closer to the heart of Upton Manor's profound mysteries, his fate irrevocably intertwined with the legacy of the ancient estate.

13

B en's desperation weighed upon him like a leaden cloak, suffocating him as he confronted the desolation of Upton Manor Wing. Annie's cryptic words had led him to this forsaken place, where she purportedly resided. Yet, as his eyes swept over the crumbling edifices and desolate surroundings, a profound sense of dread seized him, coiling around his heart like a vice.

The structures, once proud and formidable, now stood as solemn sentinels of decay, their weather beaten façades bearing the scars of time's relentless march. With every hesitant step Ben took, the weight of his expectations seemed to grow heavier, gradually eclipsed by a suffocating sense of foreboding. Each creak of the aged floorboards beneath his feet echoed like a mournful lament, further entwining him in the web of despair that seemed to pervade the very air around him.

Stepping into the first building, its once sturdy structure now reduced to a mere shell of its former grandeur, Ben's voice faltered as he tentatively called out Annie's name. Yet, the only reply he received was the haunting echo of his own voice, reverberating through the cavernous emptiness of the dilapidated walls. Each syllable seemed to hang in the air like a ghostly whisper, unanswered amidst the desolation that surrounded him.

Room after desolate room, corridor after echoing corridor, his desperate search yielded nothing but the barren embrace of emptiness. Each step forward felt like a futile dance with despair, as the silence of the abandoned halls seemed to mock him, whispering taunts of cruel indifference into the stale air. The absence of life echoed louder than any sound, a chilling reminder of his isolation in this forsaken place. Yet, undeterred by the oppressive silence, he pressed on, driven by a flicker of hope amidst the suffocating darkness.

With each heavy footfall, he trudged onward to the next building, his heart burdened by a weight he could scarcely bear. As he crossed the threshold into the dimly illuminated interior, his steps faltered, hesitating in the face of the unknown. "Annie?" he called out, the sound barely more than a fragile whisper, barely audible amidst the vast expanse of silence that enveloped him like a shroud. But the void remained unyielding, offering no solace in return, only the oppressive stillness that clung to him like a suffocating cloak, threatening to smother his fragile hopes.

As twilight descended upon the crumbling buildings, their decaying façades casting elongated shadows across the desolate landscape, Ben's desperation reached a crescendo. How could Annie have vanished without a trace? The unanswered questions gnawed at his mind like relentless beasts, clawing at the edges of his sanity. Where had she gone, in this forsaken labyrinth of ruins and solitude? The encroaching darkness seemed to mirror the bleak uncertainty that engulfed his thoughts, each fleeting moment slipping through his fingers like grains of sand in an hourglass, leaving only the hollow ache of unanswered longing in its wake.

With a heart heavy with disappointment and limbs burdened by exhaustion, he emerged from the dilapidated confines of the final building, the crushing weight of his failure threatening to consume him. Despite his relentless search, Annie remained elusive, her absence a gaping void that echoed with unanswered questions and haunting regrets. The desolation that surrounded him seemed to mirror the desolation within, each crumbling brick and shattered window a silent testament to his fruitless quest. As he stood amidst the ruins, a profound sense of loss washed over him, leaving him adrift in a sea of uncertainty and despair.

In the depths of his despair, a flicker of determination ignited within him, refusing to be extinguished by the shadows of defeat. Though his heart weighed heavy with sorrow and uncertainty, he found resolve in the unwavering promise he made to himself: he would not give up on Annie. With a new found strength coursing through his veins, he pledged to pursue her relentlessly, undeterred by the daunting odds stacked against him. Every fibre of his being resonated with the conviction that he would search for her until his very last breath, traversing every corner of the earth if need be, to unravel the mystery of her disappearance and reclaim the light that had been extinguished from his life. In the face of adversity, his determination burned bright, a beacon of hope cutting through the darkness that threatened to engulf him.

In a world fraught with uncertainty and chaos, Annie was Ben's steadfast anchor, a beacon of light in the tumultuous sea of his existence. Her absence left a void within him, a gnawing emptiness that could not be ignored. Yet, in the face of this daunting reality, he refused to succumb to despair. With a fire burning in his soul, fuelled by the depth of his love and the unwavering resolve to reclaim what was lost, he vowed to traverse every obstacle, to brave every storm until she was safely by his side once more.

With each step forward, he felt the weight of his determination propel him onward, a force stronger than any adversity that dared stand in his way. The night enveloped him in its embrace, the darkness serving not as a hindrance, but as a canvas upon which his unwavering pursuit unfolded. Guided by the faintest glimmer of hope, he chased after shadows, relentless in his quest to reunite with the one who held his heart.

Through the winding paths and treacherous terrain, Ben pressed forward, fuelled by the memories of their shared moments and the promise of a future yet unwritten. Every beat of his heart echoed with her name, a constant reminder of the love that bound them together. And as he journeyed into the unknown, he knew that no obstacle, no distance, could keep them apart, for their love was a force of nature, unyielding and eternal.

As he turned to leave, a lone glimmer of hope cut through the dense, suffocating darkness encircling him. Like a radiant beacon in a sea of shadows, it beckoned to him, offering a whisper of possibility that ignited a fervent determination within his soul. With each flicker of its light, he felt a surge of resolve coursing through him, driving him forward with unwavering purpose.

In that fleeting moment, clarity washed over him like a cleansing tide. He knew, without a shadow of doubt, that there existed only one path forward: to confront the elusive Dr. Kendal. For within the depths of the enigmatic doctor's secrets lay the potential key to finding Annie, the one he held most dear.

With every step towards this final confrontation, his heart rumbled with anticipation, his mind sharpened with focus. For he understood that within the unknown labyrinth of Dr. Kendal's domain, lay the answers he so desperately sought. And so, fuelled by the flickering flame of hope and the unwavering resolve in his heart, he ventured forth into the unknown, ready to face whatever challenges awaited him in his quest for truth and salvation.

Despite the chilling prospect of entering the annex by force, Ben refused to succumb to the creeping tendrils of fear snaking their way through his mind and body. Instead, he fortified himself against the tumultuous waves of uncertainty crashing upon him. With an unwavering resolve burning within him, he grasped the gravity of the moment, understanding that the elusive answers he desperately sought lay ensconced within the forbidden confines of that mysterious domain.

Every sinew in his body pulsed with a sense of purpose as he embraced the urgency of the situation. He knew that time was not a luxury he could afford to squander. The quest to unravel the truth and reclaim his cherished Annie demanded his utmost courage and determination.

Summoning his inner strength, he drew in a deep breath, grounding himself for the daunting odyssey that lay ahead.

With a merciless resolve coursing through his veins, he steeled himself against the perils awaiting him on the treacherous path towards revelation and reunion.

As he advanced towards the imposing façade of Upton Manor, each footfall seemed to bear the increasing burden of his purpose upon his shoulders. Yet, even as the weight threatened to crush his resolve, he remained steadfast in his determination. Within the shadowy recesses of those ancient walls, he sensed a mystery: the promise of salvation intertwined with the looming spectre of damnation. Despite the palpable dread gnawing at his insides, he refused to retreat from the path that destiny had laid before him.

With a heart ablaze with resolve, he braced himself for the impending confrontation, knowing full well that the depths of darkness he was about to confront held both peril and possibility in equal measure. He understood that to hesitate now would be to forsake the chance to bring Annie back into the light, a risk he could not afford to take.

Armed with an unyielding spirit and an indomitable will, he embraced the unknown with open arms, ready to brave whatever malevolent forces lurked within those foreboding walls. For the love of Annie, he would confront any darkness, endure any trial, and make any sacrifice required to see her safely returned home.

14

The bitter chill of the night air enveloped Ben like a shroud. The moon hung high, casting eerie shadows that danced across the landscape. Despite the late hour, there was an urgency in his movements, a determination that drove him forward through the stillness of the night.

With each step, gravel crunched beneath his boots, the sound echoing through the silence like a solitary heartbeat in the vast expanse of night. His destination loomed ahead – the old shed, its weathered exterior a testament to years gone by, standing solitary amidst the overgrown foliage that surrounded it.

As he approached, the shed seemed to loom larger, its presence commanding respect even in its state of disrepair. He reached for the handle, feeling the rough texture of rusted metal beneath his fingertips. With a steady push, he swung the door open, the hinges protesting with a loud creak that shattered the stillness of the night.

Inside, the darkness was suffocating, swallowing everything in its path. He reached for the switch, flicking it on with a sense of relief as light flooded the small space. Dust danced in the air, catching the glow of the solitary bulb that hung from the ceiling.

His gaze swept over the tools that lined the walls – rusty saws, worn hammers, and an assortment of other implements that had long since lost their lustre. But there, in the corner, leaning against the wall, was the object of his search – the axe.

Its handle was worn smooth with use, the blade gleaming dully in the artificial light. His fingers closed around the familiar grip, the weight of the tool reassuring in his hands. He knew what he had to do.

As he made his way back to the manor, the weight of the axe seemed to anchor him to the earth, grounding him in the reality of the task ahead. Inside, the air felt heavy, laden with an unspoken tension that seemed to seep from the very walls.

He moved through the hallway with purpose, his footsteps echoing in the silence. There were memories here, buried beneath layers of dust and neglect – memories of happier times, of laughter and love. But there were shadows too, lurking in the corners, whispering secrets that refused to be forgotten.

Stopping before the closed door to the annex, he took a deep breath, steadying himself for what lay beyond. He called out, his voice cutting through the quiet, "Dr. Kendal. Dr. Kendal." The words hung in the air, but there was no reply, only the haunting echo of his own voice. A sense of foreboding settled upon him as he waited, each passing moment stretching into an eternity. The stillness of the house seemed to amplify the absence of any response. Dr. Kendal's whereabouts remained a mystery, concealed behind the solid barrier of the door.

Impatience gnawed at Ben, urging him to take action. Gripping the axe tighter, he decided to take matters into his own hands. The cold metal of the tool met the doorknob with a resounding thud as he struck it. And with each blow, he drew closer to the truth, to the answers he so desperately sought. With each swing of the axe, he felt the weight of the past bearing down on him, a burden too heavy to bear alone. But he knew that he had to keep going, that he couldn't turn back now. For behind that door lay the key to unlocking the mysteries. A shiver ran down his spine, a mix of anticipation and uncertainty, as he repeated the action until the knob yielded.

The door swung open, revealing a dimly lit hallway that led to the annex. Ben cautiously stepped into the shadows, his senses on high alert. The air was heavy with an indescribable tension, as though the very walls held secrets that begged to be uncovered.

As he cautiously ventured forward, the eerie creak of an ancient rocking chair echoed through the stillness, setting his nerves on edge. Slowly, the silhouette of a weathered old man materialized from the enveloping shadows, ensconced within the worn embrace of the rocking chair. The room itself appeared suspended in a timeless limbo, every corner cloaked in a silent history, while the feeble light struggled to unveil the rugged contours of the man's visage, etched with the stories of a lifetime.

"Dr. Kendal?" Ben's voice trembled with a mixture of relief and concern.

The old man remained still, his gaze fixed on some distant point. The lines etched on his face told tales of time and hardship, and a heavy silence hung in the air, as if the room itself held its breath, waiting for the next revelation.

Dr. Kendal, a once-respected figure in the community, now sat before Ben, his haunted eyes revealing the torment that plagued his soul.

"Dr. Kendal? Dr. Kendal, are you listening to me?" Ben's voice cut through the oppressive silence.

"You've had all you want of this," Dr. Kendal replied, his words carrying a heavy resignation. "I knew you would come looking for me eventually."

His gaze seemed to pierce through the veil of time, haunted by a past he could no longer escape. "You're not the only one. The shadow demons. They want to take me to hell for what I've done."

Ben's eyes widened. "What have you done, Dr. Kendal?"

"I've sinned," the doctor confessed, his voice barely audible.

"We've all sinned," Ben offered, attempting to provide some solace.

"Not like me. I've sinned in the worst possible way," Dr Kendal said.

"Murder?" Ben asked.

"As good as," he replied.

Ben felt a chill crawl up his spine. "Tell me. Please."

Dr. Kendal's gaze met Ben's, and for a moment, he saw the struggle etched on the doctor's face.

Dr Kendal said. "Twenty years ago... I lived here with my imaginary twin, my other self, Andrew. We were very happy."

Ben listened intently as Dr. Kendal unfolded a tale of love and jealousy, woven into the fabric of a tragic past. "Then one day... Andrew fell in love with a young maiden from Fish Town. I was confused. The Andrew part of me was very much in love, but the Adrian part of me was very jealous."

The room seemed to close in as he continued, revealing the sinister turn of events. "I prayed to God to help me. But God didn't listen. I had to get rid of Andrew's girlfriend and put the blame on him. So the Adrian side of me convinced Andrew to take the girl to Sharkham Point and push her off the cliff then make it look as if both of them had made a lover's pact and committed suicide by throwing themselves off the cliff."

Ben's breath caught as he tried to grasp the gravity of the revelation.

"Her body was found on the rocks below, but of course, Andrew was never found, so the police assumed his body had been washed out to sea." Dr. Kendal continued. "After Andrew died, this place was never the same."

A moment of realization struck Ben.

"How can Andrew be dead when he never existed? That young lady was your girlfriend, so it wasn't an accident, was it?" he asked.

Dr. Kendal's gaze held a mixture of guilt and horror. "No. I saw her face as he pushed her over the cliff. I saw his face as well. It wasn't the face of my twin; it was the face of pure evil. He wanted to kill that young girl."

Ben pressed further. "Andrew didn't kill her. You killed her. But who are you? Adrian or Andrew?"

"Who do you think I am?" he asked. "His girlfriend was so young. She had her whole life ahead of her. I had to consider things. I decided not to involve the police."

"Why the hell not?" Ben asked.

"I couldn't see the point," he replied. "If I'd reported an accident to the police, they would have been bound to find out the truth. I couldn't take that chance. I felt Andrew was a good person at heart. He'd made a mistake. And let the evil in. Satan is a sly entity, and can influence any of us in a moment of weakness."

Ben's mind reeled as he tried to process the darkness that unfolded before him. "Tell me, what happened next?"

"I went to live in Scotland to forget about what had happened," Dr. Kendal replied.

"But the dead girl, she must have had some family who were looking for her, no?" asked Ben.

"She was an only child who had run away from home. She hadn't talked to her parents in ages. No one was going to come looking for her," he replied.

"This girl who died...she haunts this place, doesn't she?" Ben asked.

Dr. Kendal's eyes widened. "She's not the only one. The shadow demons are looking for me. They're always looking."

Ben, now entrapped in a web of the supernatural, sought clarification. "Who the hell are the shadow demons, Dr. Kendal?"

"The shadow demons are the entities of this manor," he replied. "After Andrew murdered his girlfriend, the demons tormented me. Now they lie in wait. Waiting for my secret to come out. That's why I'm locked in here. I pray to God every day to protect me. But God won't, so what hope is there for me? The only one who looks after me now is my niece."

Ben's brow furrowed. "Where's your niece now, Dr. Kendal?"

"I've unburdened myself, but I'm still her uncle," he replied.

"This girl who died...what was her name, Dr. Kendal?" Ben asked.

"Her name was...Annie. Annie Tolcher," he replied. "She's buried in St. Mary's churchyard."

Ben, incredulous, struggled to comprehend the truth. "There must be some mistake."

"No mistake. I saw her die. With my own eyes," he said.

"Oh, God!" said Ben.

"There's no God here any more. This manor is just full of evil. You should leave! Leave now!" Dr. Kendal cried out.

Ben hesitated, torn between the inexplicable and the rational. "What about you, Dr. Kendal?"

"I must accept...my fate. Have the shadow demons come for me? I'm ready," he replied.

Just as the shadows of despair threatened to engulf the room, a soft voice echoed through the darkness. "Uncle."

"Eleanor?" Dr. Kendal asked.

"Yes," the voice replied. A slender figure emerged from the shadows, revealing Eleanor. She cast a sympathetic glance at Ben, her eyes betraying a mixture of sorrow and understanding.

"I'm sorry, my dear. I had to tell him. I can't live with it any more," Dr. Kendal confessed to her.

She placed a reassuring hand on his shoulder. "It's okay. Now, come on. You should be in bed. It's late."

Ben, still grappling with the revelations, couldn't help but say, " You are Mrs. Parkes, the caretaker."

"Don't be silly. I knew someone would find out sooner or later. It was just a matter of time," she replied with a weary smile.

"I'm so sorry, my dear. But now the shadow demons are calling me. I can't take it to the grave, or God won't save my soul," Dr. Kendal said, his voice laden with resignation.

Mrs. Parkes, ever the pillar of strength, comforted him. "Don't worry about that now. You just get some rest. You deserve it."

As the room descended into a heavy silence, the lines between guilt and redemption blurred, and Ben found himself standing on the precipice of a reality where the darkness of the past intertwined with the shadows of the present. The mysteries that lay ahead seemed to echo the shadow demons that haunted Dr. Kendal's tormented soul.

As she gently led him away, Ben was left alone in the oppressive silence of the room.

The echoes of Dr. Kendal's confession lingered, like an unsettling melody playing in the background of a chilling tale. Ben's mind swirled with a maelstrom of emotions, grappling with the weight of the revelation and the unsettling presence that seemed to permeate the very walls of the manor.

As Mrs. Parkes tenderly tucked Dr. Kendal into the comforting embrace of his bed, her façade of kindness concealed a chilling agenda lurking beneath her serene demeanour. With a cold, calculated determination, she seized a pillow, the innocuous object transformed into a weapon of lethal intent. The rhythmic rise and fall of her hands betrayed no hesitation as she pressed the pillow down, silencing the feeble protests of the old man, snuffing out the dwindling flame of life within him. In the hushed darkness of the night, the stillness itself bore witness to her treacherous deed, her hands now tainted with the damning mark of betrayal, forever stained by the blood of her transgression.

Armed with the axe left behind by Ben, she went into the room where he was standing in thought, her footsteps echoing in the darkness like a harbinger of doom. Meanwhile, he was met with a violent confrontation as her wrath manifested in the swing of the deadly weapon.

With each swing of the axe, she drew closer, her eyes ablaze with a madness that knew no bounds.

Fate intervened as Ben narrowly evaded the final blow, retreating to the safety of his room with a heart pounding with fear. Hiding beneath the bed offered little sanctuary as her presence loomed over him, her eyes gleaming with a twisted satisfaction.

He waited in silence, his breath held tight as he listened to her footsteps fade away. Only when he was certain she'd gone he dared to slide out from under the bed, his heart pounding against his ribs like a caged bird desperate for escape.

But his moment of relief was short-lived. As he got up, he saw her silhouette against the dim light, axe raised high above her head. Instinct took over, and he rolled to the side, narrowly avoiding the deadly blow. With adrenaline coursing through his veins, he seized her legs, sending her crashing to the floor.

Battling against the suffocating grip of fear that threatened to consume him whole, he found himself locked in a primal struggle, his fingers coiling around her throat with a grip forged from the depths of desperation. Each heartbeat pounded in his ears like a relentless drumbeat of terror, urging him to fight or flee, yet he remained rooted in place, driven by an urgency that brooked no hesitation.

With every fibre of his being straining against the overwhelming tide of panic, he felt her frantic movements beneath him, a wild symphony of thrashing limbs and gasping breaths. Yet, he could not yield. He could not relent. For in that fleeting moment of turmoil, every shred of his resolve crystallized into a singular purpose.

The darkness of uncertainty loomed large around him, but within the crucible of his own turmoil, he clung fiercely to the belief that he must persevere, that he must emerge victorious against the looming spectre of fear. And so, with trembling hands and a heart heavy with dread, he pressed on, driven by the unyielding force of his own determination.

And then, mercifully, she went limp.

Shock coursed through him as he released his grip, recoiling from what he'd done. Horror twisted his features as he stared down at her unconscious form. How did it come to this? How did he become a participant in this nightmare?

He reached for the axe, fingers trembling as they wrapped around the handle. For a moment, he held it aloft, the weight of it heavy in his grasp. But then, with a shuddering breath, he lowered it, his resolve faltering in the face of the carnage around him.

Leaving the room behind, he stepped on to the landing, the weight of his actions bearing down on him like a leaden cloak. He stood there, consumed by grief and guilt, his gaze fixed on the ceiling above as if searching for answers in the shadows.

But before he could find solace in the silence, a presence stirred behind him. Slowly, he turned, dread pooling in the pit of his stomach as he faced Mrs. Parkes once more. With a glint of malice in her eyes as she inched closer, her intentions clear.

Without a second thought, he reacted, the axe in his hand moving with a speed born of desperation. With a swift, brutal motion, the blade found its mark with sickening accuracy. For a moment, there was only the sound of her gasp, the echo of her pain, before she crumpled to the ground at his feet.

Shaken to the core, he staggered away, his steps unsteady as he descended into the dark cellar below. Cobwebs brushed against his skin like icy fingers as he moved, each step a struggle against the weight of his guilt.

A new presence emerged from the shadows. Annie, her eyes brimming with tears, appeared before him in the dim light. Their conversation was brief yet laden with emotion, the weight of the past hanging heavy between them. A single tear fell from his left eye as he gazed upon her, a silent acknowledgement of the pain they both carried.

She stood frozen, her heart pounding against her chest, as the words hung heavy in the air between them.

"So, now you know," she whispered, her voice barely audible.

His eyes widened in disbelief. "Why didn't you tell me?" he asked, his voice tinged with hurt and confusion.

"I couldn't," she confessed, her gaze dropping to the ground. "I didn't want to lose you."

Their conversation echoed in the stillness, each word laden with unspoken truths and hidden fears.

"Why didn't you tell me about Dr. Kendal and his niece?" his voice was a mixture of anguish and frustration.

She swallowed hard, her throat tight with emotion. "I was scared the shadow demons would come for me too."

The weight of her confession hung heavy in the air, casting a pall over their tender moment.

"You know, I...I love you," he admitted, his voice breaking with emotion.

Tears welled up in her eyes as she met his gaze, her heart aching with the intensity of her feelings. "I love you too."

But even as their love bound them together, she knew that sometimes love required sacrifice. Sometimes love meant letting go.

"But when you love someone, you have to set them free," she whispered, her voice barely a whisper.

"Please don't go," his voice desperate and pleading.

She closed her eyes, her heart breaking with each word. "I have to."

And with those final words, a bright light pierced the darkness, illuminating her form as she stepped back and vanished before his eyes.

Left alone in the darkness once more, Ben sighed, his heart heavy with the weight of what had transpired. Annie's presence lingered in his mind, a bitter-sweet reminder of the bonds they had forged amidst the darkness.

15

As he stepped out from the grandeur of Upton Manor, the weight of its history seemed to linger in the air, swirling around him like a thick mist. With the manuscript of his latest book, The Haunting of Upton Manor, cradled securely under his arm, Ben found himself pausing, compelled to cast one last glance back at the fading silhouette of the imposing structure.

The manor, with its weathered stone walls and centuries old secrets, stood as a silent sentinel against the backdrop of the setting sun. Its windows, like watchful eyes, seemed to follow Ben's every move, hinting at the countless stories etched within its walls.

In that fleeting moment, as the evening hues painted the sky with streaks of gold and crimson, He couldn't help but feel a sense of reverence for the place that had inspired his literary endeavours. Yet, mingled with that reverence was a tinge of relief—a feeling of liberation from the confines of the manor's oppressive embrace.

With a final nod of acknowledgement to the fading silhouette, he turned away, his mind already racing with ideas for his next literary venture. For in the pages of his manuscript lay not just a story, but a testament to the enduring allure of Upton Manor and the mysteries that lay hidden within its shadows.

With a heart weighed down by the burden of betrayal, each step towards the letterbox at the end of the driveway felt like a journey through the depths of his own remorse. The keys, heavy in his trembling hand, seemed to symbolize not just the relinquishment of access but the surrender of a piece of his own shattered trust.

As he stood before the yawning mouth of the letterbox, its darkened interior swallowing the metal with a hollow clink, he couldn't shake the feeling of finality that washed over him. It was as if by dropping those keys, he was not just leaving behind a mere building, but a part of himself—the part that had once believed in the sanctity of loyalty and the resilience of love.

The countryside of Devon, with its rolling hills and verdant meadows, stretched out before him like a welcoming embrace. Yet, even amidst the tranquil beauty of nature, he couldn't escape the echoes of Upton Manor, its haunting legacy trailing behind him like a shadow.

As he drove away, the winding roads of Devon twisting like ribbons beneath his tyres, he couldn't help but glance in the rear view mirror, half expecting to see the ghostly visage of the manor looming in the distance. But all he saw was the fading silhouette of a past he could never reclaim, disappearing over the horizon.

And so, with each mile that stretched between him and Upton Manor, he found himself slowly shedding the weight of betrayal, his soul beginning to stir with the faint promise of renewal. For though the shadows of the manor may have haunted him, they could never extinguish the flicker of hope that burned within his heart, guiding him towards a future untainted by the ghosts of the past.

Meanwhile, back at the manor a lone figure materialized—a woman, her silhouette framed against the wooden patio furniture.

In the cool embrace of the mist, she indulged in languid puffs from a cigarette. Grey wisps of smoke meandered away, entwining with the ethereal tendrils, as if whispering secrets to the ancient oaks that stood sentinel in the garden.

The woman's attire, a black trouser-and-jacket ensemble paired with a crisp white blouse, exuded a professional air that resonated with the surroundings. She discarded the cigarette with a nonchalant grace, extinguishing its glow under the heel of her shoe as the man approached.

"You found the place all right, then?" she asked, extending her hand.

THE END

Also by David J Cooper

Paranormal Mystery Series
The Witch Board
The House of Dolls
The Devil's Coins
The Mirror
The Key
The Reveal

Standalone
The Devil Knows
Se Acabo La Fiesta
Cold Fury
Deadly Encounter
House on the Hill
Diana, Another Royal Scandal
Hanratty - The Final Curtain
The Haunting of Upton Manor

Watch for more at davidjcooperauthorblog.wordpress.com.

About the Author

David J Cooper, a British author, delves into the realms of the paranormal, horror, suspense, and mystery with an expert touch. Originating from Darlaston, West Midlands, his diverse journey from engineering to teaching and local politics has imbued his writing with a rich tapestry of experiences.

His literary venture began with an unforgettable mark—a featured poem, "God's Garden," acclaimed in the Best Poems and Poets of 2012 anthology. Currently residing in a tranquil Mexican town, David shares his home with four loyal dogs—Chula, Sooty, Benji and Princessa — and a vibrant parrot named Muchacho.

David's novels are an enigmatic treat for those with a taste for the eerie and the unexpected. With a knack for weaving gripping suspense and unforeseen twists, his narratives promise an enthralling journey that beckons fans of authors like Stephen King.

Read more at davidjcooperauthorblog.wordpress.com.